"Ours will not be a marriage in name only.

"You will sleep with me anytime I want, and anyplace I want."

"That is a marriage in name only, Heath. Without a relationship to back it up, sex alone doesn't make a marriage," Ann said.

"Giving advice to the lovelorn now? Why don't you write a column for the papers?"

"I see why you want to marry me, why torturing me outside the bonds of holy matrimony wouldn't be sufficient for you. It's all part of the master plan, isn't it? The plan to show everyone that the poor boy from the wrong side of the tracks has made good. It has nothing to do with me—I'm just a means to an end."

"It has *everything* to do with you," he said quietly. "Make no mistake about that."

Dear Reader,

This month marks the advent of something very special in Intimate Moments. We call it "Intimate Moments Extra," and books bearing this flash will be coming your way on an occasional basis in the future. These are books we think are a bit different from our usual, a bit longer or grittier perhaps. And our lead-off "extra" title is one terrific read. It's called *Into Thin Air*, and it's written by Karen Leabo, making her debut in the line. It's a tough look at a tough subject, but it's also a top-notch romance. Read it and you'll see what I mean.

The rest of the month's books are also terrific. We're bringing you Doreen Owens Malek's newest, *Marriage in Name Only*, as well as Laurey Bright's *A Perfect Marriage*, a very realistic look at how a marriage can go wrong before finally going very, very right. Then there's Kylie Brant's *An Irresistible Man*, a sequel to her first-ever book, *McLain's Law*, as well as Barbara Faith's sensuous and suspenseful *Moonlight Lady*. Finally, welcome Kay David to the line with *Desperate*. Some of you may have seen her earlier titles, written elsewhere as Cay David.

Six wonderful authors and six wonderful books. I hope you enjoy them all.

Yours,

Leslie Wainger
Senior Editor and Editorial Coordinator

Please address questions and book requests to:
Silhouette Reader Service
U.S.: 3010 Walden Ave., P.O. Box 1325, Buffalo, NY 14269
Canadian: P.O. Box 609, Fort Erie, Ont. L2A 5X3

MARRIAGE IN NAME ONLY

DOREEN OWENS MALEK

Published by Silhouette Books
America's Publisher of Contemporary Romance

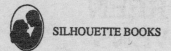

SILHOUETTE BOOKS

ISBN 0-373-07620-7

MARRIAGE IN NAME ONLY

DOREEN OWENS MALEK

is a former attorney who decided on her current career when she sold her fledgling novel to the first editor who read it. Since then, she has gained recognition for her writing, winning honors from *Romantic Times* magazine and the coveted Golden Medallion award from the Romance Writers of America. She has traveled extensively throughout Europe, but it was in her home state of New Jersey that she met and married her college sweetheart. They now live in Pennsylvania.

Chapter 1

As soon as Ann stepped off the plane, she knew she was in Florida.

She had not been home for eleven years, but the combination of humid air, salt smell and intense, direct sunlight was still as familiar to her as her own hands. She did not need to see the palm trees or sapodillas, the hibiscus or jacaranda, to know that the Keys were once again exerting their spell, even though the last time she left she fully expected never to be back again.

She stopped off in a rest room at the airport before picking up her rental car, and the mirror showed her a pretty but tired woman with striking features and circles under her wide green eyes. She brushed out her long blond hair, delicately dabbed powder on her nose and chin, and replenished her lipstick. No wonder she looked exhausted. She had been on the phone with her half brother's lawyers until the wee hours for several days—since she'd been in Europe she'd had to accommodate the time difference—and once she had returned to New York, she'd booked a flight to Florida immediately.

The problem could not wait.

Her half brother was bankrupt and had run the family business into the ground. Ann's family, the Talbots, had once been among the richest and most influential on Lime island. Now the Talbot company, a computer software supplier called Script-Soft, was on the ropes, filing for Chapter Eleven, and her half brother Tim owed money to casinos in Las Vegas, Reno, Atlantic City, and Monte Carlo. He could no longer borrow from company funds to pay his debts, since there was nothing left. In desperation, the filing attorney had tracked Ann down in Italy, where she was doing research for a new book, to tell her what was happening.

And now here she was in Florida, to deal with the crisis.

Ann had wanted nothing to do with the family business. She had not spoken to her father since she'd left, and so when he'd died he had transferred the company to Tim. But Ann still held a large portion of the stock, even though it was now valued at very little, and as Tim's sole sibling she had been consulted on the resolution of the problem.

Ann's half brother had just been arrested in Miami on federal charges of stock manipulation. He was being prosecuted for misrepresenting the financial status of ScriptSoft by issuing falsified quarterly reports in previous years. As a result of these reports, the company stock went up temporarily, allowing Tim to cash in his personal shares at a large profit. But when the company's true status was later revealed, the reconciliation by the accounting team brought in by the board of directors drove the company into bankruptcy.

Ann knew that Tim had lost the money gambling; he had a long-standing habit for which he'd gone through rehabilitation several times—to no avail. Now, apparently, there wasn't even enough money left to pay his bail.

Ann put her comb back into her purse and sighed. She loved Tim for their shared childhood, for the memories she had of the shy, lonely little boy who would visit Florida from his mother's home in New England for the summers. But since his college days she'd known he'd had a gambling problem. She had closed her eyes to his problem, never questioned him about the company or his handling of it, all to obliterate from her mind the painful connection with her father. Now both her parents were dead, Tim was in serious trouble, and she could not ignore the situation any longer.

Ann zipped her purse closed and went out into the busy corridor to claim her car.

The breeze coming in through the car window was heavy with salt, sticky against her skin, but Ann left the window open, enjoying the change from November in New York. There the post-Thanksgiving shoppers had thronged the blustery streets and the roads were clogged, as usual, with noisy traffic. Here the streets were empty except for a few pedestrians, senior citizens walking dogs or younger people jogging lazily past the bursting shrubbery. The change in pace was jarring, especially since Ann had not experienced it for so long, but it brought back memories of still, lazy days and breathless starry nights, the endless summers on Lime Island when she was a girl.

But Ann had promised herself she wouldn't think about that. She turned purposefully down a side street, away from the business district, heading toward the water.

She had some time before her business appointment and she wanted to see her old house again. It had been sold five years earlier, when her mother had died, and at the time she had let Tim handle everything and never questioned what he'd done with the money. She hadn't cared. Now she assumed that the profit from the house had gone into his gambling. She probably should have paid more attention to his dealings, but her grief had been such that she'd wanted nothing to do with the house, the company, or anything else that had issued from her father's life. Perhaps she had been foolish, because she'd always known that Tim was weak, but her emotional survival had dictated that she cut herself off from everything in the past and start fresh. After college she had carved out a career writing historical fiction, and she had been content to support herself by living in the fictional past, until the summons from Tim's lawyer had brought her rudely back to the present.

Ann glided to a stop at the curb and stared up at the house, a white stucco Colonial with dark blue shutters set back from a wide expanse of green lawn, no mean feat to maintain through the blistering heat of a south Florida summer. Her father had installed automatic sprinklers to keep his property a verdant emerald, and one of her most vivid memories was of being awakened in the simmering summer dawns by the hiss and rush of the sprinklers outside her window. Now they were silent and she studied the expertly cultivated lush foliage, the neat brick path leading to the front door, the clapboard boat house to the left of the main dwelling, the blue waters of the canal running behind the rear patio and leading to the intracoastal waterway. A Miami millionaire owned the Talbot place now and used it only occasionally for a getaway.

Except for the ancient gardener snipping desultorily at a kudzu vine growing along the edge of the crushed stone driveway, it looked like nobody was home.

Ann put her head back against the headrest and closed her eyes. She had met Heath in that boat house, and that meeting had changed her life forever.

She gave the car gas and drove away, recalling how she had lived in that mansion with her father, Henry Talbot, and his second wife, her mother. Ann had been the daughter of privilege, sent to the best private schools, coming home to the Keys to spend the summers with her half brother Tim, the child of her father's brief first marriage. She had never given a thought to the servants, the nannies, the summer home in Maine, the condo in the Bahamas, until she had turned her back on it all when she was seventeen. Her life since then had been very different, but she hadn't missed any of the niceties associated with her father's success, just as she hadn't missed the man himself. When he'd died, she had attended his funeral in his hometown of Springfield, Massachusetts, but had left without speaking to anybody. When her mother had died a few years later, Ann had brought the body north to bury her in New Jersey with the rest of her family. And except for occasional phone calls and visits from Tim, she had buried the past along with her mother.

If Tim had managed ScriptSoft profitably, she would never have come back home again.

Ann turned a corner and headed back to the business district, crossing the railroad tracks that bisected the island. To the south of them lay Hispaniola, the Cuban-Indian shanty town where Heath had lived when she'd first met him.

She had no idea where he lived now.

Downtown Port Lisbon had changed; there were new high rises along the main street and a traffic light at the corner by Burdine's department store. Ann parked in the lot behind the refurbished Acadian-style building that housed the law firm handling Tim's bankruptcy. She glanced in the rearview mirror to tidy her hair, got out of the car and straightened the tailored jacket of the lightweight wool suit she was wearing.

She felt like she was about to face a firing squad. As she walked toward the entrance, she concentrated on the lunch she was to have with her old friend Amy later that day and forced herself through the lobby and into the elevator that led up to the lawyer's office.

Harold Caldwell's secretary ushered Ann right inside as soon as she announced her name. From Caldwell's grave expression she knew that the situation had not improved since she'd last spoken to him.

"Mr. Caldwell," Ann said, extending her hand.

"Miss Talbot. Have a seat."

Ann sat in the leather chair in his comfortable office, glancing out the picture window at the bay below and around the room at the tasteful paintings, standing plants, inlaid oak desk and Oriental rug. Caldwell shuffled a stack of papers and cleared his throat. Ann met the eyes of the lawyer, a well-groomed, graying man in his fifties wearing the traditional pin-striped suit and conservative tie.

"You know the purpose of this meeting, Miss Talbot," he finally said. "I've already told you most of what you need to hear over the phone, but there are several documents that you must sign, and also the matter of your brother's confinement. Where shall we begin?"

"I'd like to get my brother out of jail."

"Do you have fifty thousand dollars?" Caldwell asked, raising his brows inquiringly.

"No, but I thought bail could be arranged through a bondsman. Isn't that the usual practice?"

Caldwell frowned. "It's been difficult to find a bondsman to put up the money. Your brother is regarded as a flight risk."

"What?" Ann said indignantly. "That's preposterous."

Caldwell stared at her. "Apparently you aren't aware that when Tim was arrested several months ago for writing bad checks to a casino, he fled the jurisdiction."

Ann closed her eyes.

"You haven't been in very close touch with your brother, have you?" Caldwell asked gently.

"No. Not lately. He avoids talking to me when he's having ... difficulties."

"Well, he's having very severe difficulties now. Unless you can come up with the cash to foot his bail, he will probably remain where he is."

"I live in an apartment in New York, Mr. Caldwell, so I don't have equity in a home or other property to mortgage. I have a few thousand in savings and that's it."

"Your writing career is not lucrative?"

"I've just begun it, Mr. Caldwell. I was a researcher for a publishing house before I started writing. Now I'm working on my third book and my first one just came out late last year. Royalties take a long time to arrive and the advances from the publisher are just enough to live on in the meantime."

"Excuse me for being so personal, Miss Talbot, but your father was a very wealthy man. He left you nothing at all?"

"I wanted nothing, and he knew that. He left everything, the business and his real estate holdings, and all of his investments, to Tim."

"And you didn't even supervise your brother's actions?"

Ann looked away from the lawyer's probing stare. "Tim is a grown man and, for personal reasons, I wanted to be divorced from ScriptSoft and anything else associated with my father. I'm sorry if you can't understand that."

"But you must have known about your brother's problem," the lawyer insisted.

"I felt that it was his business," Ann replied shortly. "What else do we need to discuss?"

Caldwell shrugged. "I told you most of it on the phone, as I said. ScriptSoft is insolvent, the people on the board of directors are suing your brother for mismanagement, and the Securities and Exchange Commission is preparing to prosecute him for stock fraud.''

''Is there any good news?''

Caldwell sighed. ''Not much. A fresh infusion of several million dollars would save the day, allowing the present management to pay the company's debts, trim the staff, sell off the stagnant real estate and reorganize. Short of that, the bankruptcy court will take over to portion out the meager assets to the creditors, most of whom won't get very much because little is left.''

''What about Tim?''

''If he can't make bail, he will remain in jail until his trial and then he will probably be convicted and do ten to fifteen years.''

''What happens if he pleads guilty to a lesser charge? Won't that help?''

''He's still likely to do time. The courts are cracking down on these manipulators. I'm afraid the eighties are catching up with us. I'm sorry.''

Ann shook her head. ''How could this have happened to ScriptSoft? Didn't anybody else at the company know what Tim was doing?''

''He was very clever, Miss Talbot. He inflated the stock, sold it off high, and progressively drained the company. He owned the majority of the stock and as the controlling interest he had a free hand. By the time the board figured out what he was up to, it was too late. I assume from what you've just said that you were never informed or consulted about his management policies.''

"No. I owned the stock but never paid attention to the value of it. When the reports came in I threw them in a drawer."

"Because there was bad blood between you and your father?" Caldwell asked.

"Yes," Ann said crisply in a tone which indicated that Caldwell was definitely not to pursue this line of inquiry.

"I remember Henry Talbot," the lawyer mused. "He was an astute businessman, very active in this community. I played in golf tournaments with him from time to time. He had to take it easy even then—his heart was never very good."

Ann said nothing.

"I must say I'm very sorry to see his company come to this. It was once very prosperous, and your mother one of Port Lisbon's leading hostesses. She was a lovely lady and I was saddened to hear of her death."

"Thank you."

"Cancer?"

"Yes."

"Did she suffer long?"

"It seemed long."

"What a shame. She was so young."

There was a tap on Caldwell's door and Ann was grateful for the interruption of his funeral dirge on the downfall of her family. He got up to have a hastily whispered conference with his secretary, and when he came back he was holding a slip of paper and wearing a strange expression.

"What is it?" Ann asked.

"I can't believe this," Caldwell said, shaking his head. "You have a visitor, Miss Talbot. A benefactor who read about ScriptSoft's impending bankruptcy and Tim's arrest in the Miami newspapers. He says he is willing to refinance the company and pay your brother's bail in the bargain.''

"What?'' Ann said sharply, sitting up straight.

The door opened behind Caldwell and standing before her was Heath Bodine.

Chapter 2

Ann would have known him anywhere. His lush black hair was shorter, there were a few lines around his eyes and mouth, and his lean body now had the hard muscularity of full manhood, but he was just as gorgeous now as when she had last seen him.

"Hello, Ann," he said quietly, his wide, heavily lashed dark eyes fixed on hers.

Ann was stunned, speechless. She couldn't look away from him. Her heart began to pound and she put her hand to her throat.

He was wearing brown pants with a beige, raw silk sweater and the same type of leather moccasins he had favored as a youth. His dusky skin was tanned an even deeper shade of amber than she remembered and the gold watch on his wrist gleamed against it. He seemed more vibrant than her vivid memory of him, and she felt like a shadow by comparison with the vitality he brought into the room.

"Heath told my secretary that he is an old friend of yours," Caldwell said. "I imagine you have a lot to catch up on, so I'll leave you two alone. Ann, we'll talk later, I need your signature on some documents."

The lawyer was gone before Ann could say a word. She stared at Heath, her mouth dry, her palms wet, acutely conscious of her own haggard appearance and reduced circumstances.

"Are you the benefactor Mr. Caldwell mentioned?" she finally managed to whisper.

"The same."

"Is this some kind of cruel joke? Why on earth would *you* want to help me?"

"I have my reasons."

"I can just imagine what they are," Ann said bitterly.

"You don't have the first idea," he replied flatly, his eyes narrow and hard.

"Go home, Heath. I need a lot of cash and even if you had it, I wouldn't take it from you."

"Why, Princess? Is my money tainted?"

His use of his former nickname for her hurt more than she would have believed possible.

"Your money is nonexistent," she said bitingly, feeling the need to hurt him back. "You were very pretty, Heath, but very poor. That's why my father objected to you, remember?"

"Your father objected to the fact that my old man was a drunk and my mother the friendliest woman in town, not to mention that less than desirable Seminole blood flowing through my veins. But that didn't matter to you when we were between the sheets, did it, Princess?"

"Let's not do this to each other, Heath," Ann whispered, swallowing hard. He had hardly been with her a minute and already they were drawing blood.

"Why not? Is it too late to tell the truth?"

"It's too late for everything."

"But not too late to write a check. You've been out of touch, Annie, I'm not the same lowlife you left behind in Hispaniola when you skipped town."

Ann heard the flinty edge in his voice, saw the steel gleam in his eyes. "Must we play this game? I know you hate me, Heath, so exactly what are you doing here?" she asked wearily.

"I'm here to save your bacon, Annie. Isn't that what one old friend should do for another?"

"We were never friends."

"We were much more than that," he said in a low tone, holding her gaze.

Ann looked away from him. "Do you have seven million dollars?" she asked in a scoffing tone.

"Yes."

She looked back at him in amazement. He was completely serious.

"Find that hard to believe, do you, rich girl?" he said sarcastically. "Oh, excuse me, I guess that term doesn't apply to you anymore, does it?"

"There's no point to this exercise, Heath. You've obviously come to torture me but you will have to get in line. My brother and all of his creditors are way ahead of you."

"Don't you want to hear my generous offer?"

"No."

"You don't think I mean it, do you? Well, I do, and I have the money."

"How did you get it?"

"Ah, so you *are* curious. Do you think I stole it?"

Ann didn't answer.

"That would be in line with the Talbot opinion of me, wouldn't it?" he said nastily. "Though it seems your brother is more into larceny than I am these days."

That was a low and calculated blow, and Ann bit her lip, still saying nothing.

He stared hard at her, then seemed to relent, looking down pensively and then up again at her face.

"You recall I was always good around boats. Anyway, after you left me at the altar, so to speak, I joined the navy. While working for Uncle Sam I invented a new type of sealing valve that prevents water from getting into a boat's motor, and I later sold the patent to a private company for several million dollars."

Ann listened, astonished that she had never heard about this upward turn in his fortunes.

"I invested the money in Bimini Boat Works, and built it into a multi-outlet facility with marinas all over the Keys and mainland Florida."

"*You're* Bimini Boat Works?" Ann said incredulously. She had seen the company's billboards and advertisements everywhere since she returned to Florida.

"I take it nobody told you," he replied flatly, reading her stunned expression.

"I don't think anybody knew. My mother's been dead for five years and my brother Tim hasn't been in Florida much since my father passed away. He ran ScriptSoft from Massachusetts."

"Ran it into the ground, you mean. And you haven't exactly been in touch, have you?" he said with a thin smile. "Couldn't wait to scrape Hispaniola from the soles of your shoes, Princess?"

"That isn't fair, Heath. I didn't want to see anybody. My memories of Port Lisbon were...very painful."

"Oh, not as painful as mine, lady," he said softly, watching her face. "Not as painful as mine. *I* was the one who got dumped, remember?"

"You don't know what happened, Heath. You never heard the full story," Ann protested.

"Oh, I'm sure you've got some lovely explanation all worked out, something classy and reasonable to satisfy your delicate conscience. You wouldn't want to think of yourself as a woman who would lead a man on to the brink of distraction and then ditch him for a better deal, would you? You could never live with that." He leaned against Caldwell's desk, folding his arms and crossing his legs at the ankle in a characteristic posture.

"You won't believe anything I say, so why should I try? You just want to enjoy my downfall and your corresponding triumph."

"Quite a reversal of fortunes, isn't it, Princess?" Heath said softly, a dangerous light in his eyes that Ann recalled very well. He had looked like that when her father had threatened to separate them, all those years ago.

"I can see that you're savoring every second of it."

"Tell me Annie," he said tauntingly, "would you have called me up for a loan if you'd known I was flush?"

"Go to hell," Ann said.

"Ah, that's my girl. I don't know what you've been doing while your brother was pissing away your company but it obviously hasn't killed your spirit entirely."

"So that's why you're here?" she said dully. "To witness my humiliation?"

"Partly."

"Well, you've done so. Now you can go."

"But I'm not finished yet. Don't you want to hear my generous offer?"

"No."

"I see. It's okay with you if your dissolute brother remains behind bars? I can get him out, you know. I can get him out and hire the best lawyers to defend him. They'll help him to plead reduced capacity because of his gambling addiction. He might not spend a minute more in jail."

"What do you want?"

"I'll get to that."

"Tell me *now*."

"All in good time. I can also save ScriptSoft, buy the majority interest and open up the cash flow to pump up the stock price. The ScriptSoft scandal would vanish from the papers, and the board of directors would get happy. They might even drop the charges against your brother, who knows? It's possible the SEC could go easy on him if the company shows recovery, what do you think?"

"What do you want, Heath?" Ann said again, tightly, barely able to speak.

"I want you to marry me."

Ann stood abruptly and tried to push past him. He grabbed her arm and held her in a viselike grip.

"Let me go."

He didn't move. "I can remember a time when my touch was not so repulsive to you," he said silkily.

"I said, let me go, or I'll scream for Caldwell,"
Ann vowed, struggling silently as his fingers dug into
her wrist.

"Do you think I would care?" he said. "After
waiting all this time to see you in this position, do you
think I would actually give a damn?"

Ann yanked hard and he released her abruptly at
the same time so that she stumbled. He watched, re-
fusing to aid her, as she grabbed a plant stand and
righted herself. She paused breathlessly for several
seconds before saying, "I don't know what position
you imagine I am in, Heath, but I'm certainly not
desperate enough to marry you and fulfill your most
elaborate revenge fantasies. I know you would love to
make me dependent on you and force me to pay every
day of my life for what you think I did to you."

"What I *know* you did to me, Princess," he said
softly. "And regardless of my possible motives, do
you have any choice but to accept my offer?"

"I always have a choice," Ann said proudly.

"Really? Do you know what will happen to your
brother if he remains in prison? As I recall, he looks
a lot like you. The cons really love to get their hands
on those blond and beautiful types. It's their favorite
kind of fresh meat."

Ann looked sick.

"You were quite close to Tim when you were kids,
weren't you? I seem to remember that you were very
fond of him."

"Shut up," she said.

"It's a shame he was so weak, isn't it? Maybe it was
because your daddy gave him everything, including
his company. When you have to earn every dime
yourself, you're not likely to throw it away at the

gambling tables. Timmy got quite a reputation as an easy mark, did you know that?''

"And you just sat around waiting for this to happen, waiting to spring your trap, didn't you?" Ann said bitterly.

"I certainly kept track of the situation."

"How did you know I was here?"

"I had a detective follow you from the airport."

She stared at him. "You knew I was flying in today?"

"I've been tracking your movements for some time. I knew you would have to come back here sooner or later to deal with this debacle—I've been reading all the stock reports and stories about it in the papers. I also knew that Harold Caldwell was the bankruptcy lawyer, so the rest was easy."

"Caldwell doesn't know what you're proposing, does he?" Ann asked, shocked.

"He only knows that I've made an offer of help."

"But not the condition attached?"

"No."

"I thought not. He's far too honorable a person to go along with such a scheme."

"Unlike dishonorable Bodine, the scum of the earth, whose motives are base but whose money is green."

"This discussion is over, Heath. I'm leaving."

"Don't be so hasty, Princess. You won't get a better offer any time soon."

"Nothing on this earth would induce me to marry you, Heath, so get out of my way."

He didn't budge, merely reached for his wallet and produced a card, which he extended to her.

"Call me when you change your mind," he said.

She ignored his proferred hand and stared at him, waiting for him to let her pass.

"You'll need the number," he said warningly.

"I won't need it. Now if you don't move this instant I'll pick up the phone and call the police."

He grinned. "I own the police. The Talbots don't run Port Lisbon anymore. I do."

She picked up a silver letter opener from Caldwell's desk and held it out in front of her, blade first.

Heath laughed. "Are you going to stab me with that thing, Annie?"

"If necessary," she replied grimly.

He took an elaborate sidestep and bowed, letting her pass to the door of the office.

"I'll wait to hear from you," he called after her as she went through it.

"You'll have to wait a long time," Ann replied. She kept on moving.

"Miss Talbot, are you leaving? Mr. Caldwell wanted to see you again," the secretary said as Ann rushed past her.

"Tell him I'll call him later," Ann muttered, and bolted for the hall. Once there she leaned against the wall and closed her eyes, waiting for her heartbeat to return to normal.

Ann felt that she could barely make it to her car and she knew that she was incapable of driving. When she was steady enough to walk, she went down to the lobby of the building and called a cab to take her to her lunch meeting with Amy Horton at the Lime Island Inn. She really wanted to skip it, but she knew Amy would be waiting and she wasn't rude enough to disappoint an old friend. When the cab arrived, she sank into the back seat with relief, grateful that she didn't have to do anything but sit until she reached her destination.

Heath watched from a window of Caldwell's building as Ann climbed into a taxi and sped away. He knew that she had driven herself to the meeting with the lawyer and he took a grim satisfaction in the fact that she was now too upset to drive.

Good. She would be a lot more upset by the time he got through with her.

His handsome face was set in stone as he turned away.

Amy's welcoming smile faded as she rose from her seat in the inn's restaurant and caught sight of Ann's face. She came around the table hastily and took both of Ann's hands in hers.

"Annie, my God, what happened? You look like death. Did you have an accident?"

"In a way. I just saw Heath."

Amy's expression changed again as she pulled out a chair for her friend and then sat herself. Amy was impeccably turned out, as usual, her crisp linen suit and ruffled blouse complemented by the gold jewelry and Italian leather pumps she wore. But Amy's mind was not on her appearance at the moment. Ann was white as boiled rice and seemed to be in shock.

"You knew about him, didn't you?" Ann said to her.

"Knew what?"

"Amy, come on. Don't play dumb."

"You mean, that he became Mr. Megabucks and now owns half of Port Lisbon? Yes, I knew."

"Why didn't you ever tell me?"

Amy stared at her. "Ann, for years you burst into tears at the mere mention of his name. Everyone who knew your past history with him learned to avoid the subject completely. And then with all this recent trouble about your brother and ScriptSoft, I was hardly going to regale you with tales of Heath's good fortune while your family's company was going down the tubes."

Ann looked across the table at her boarding school roommate, whom she had known since they were both fourteen. Amy came from nearby Key Largo and had been living for the past few years in Miami, where she was a fashion buyer for a chain of retail stores. She had been Ann's closest confidante during that summer Ann had fallen in love with Heath, spending many nights covering for her friend while Ann sneaked out to tryst with her forbidden lover. Amy knew the whole story, and it had created an enduring bond between the two women that held them still. Although Ann met Amy infrequently, they spoke often by phone and each time they saw one another, it was as if their last meeting had been only hours earlier.

Amy knew what a devastating blow seeing Heath must have been to her friend. Ann had never gotten over his loss and to see him now, after so many years, when he was prospering and she was staggering from the blow of her brother's disgrace, had to be humiliating.

Amy put her hand over Ann's on the table.

"I'm so sorry," Amy said quietly. "Was it awful?"

"You can't imagine."

"How does he look? Gorgeous, I suppose."

"Yes."

"I've seen his pictures in the Miami papers. If you hadn't been off in Europe researching your books for God knows how long you'd know that he's become quite the big man locally."

"I live in New York, Amy. Even when I'm home I don't get much news from Florida."

"Well, he's been living it up, donating money everywhere, attending charity balls, shaking hands and writing checks. I guess you can't blame him, to come from Hispaniola and wind up one of the wealthiest men in the state is quite an achievement. And all by the age of thirty. Where did you see him, anyway?"

"In Caldwell's office."

"What was he doing there?"

"He came to make me an offer."

Amy paused with her water glass halfway to her lips. "An offer?" she echoed.

"He said he would bail Timmy out of jail and pay off ScriptSoft's debts if I would marry him."

Amy put the glass down, staring at Ann. A waiter appeared at her elbow and said, "Can I get you ladies anything to drink?"

"I'll take a double Scotch on the rocks," Amy said rapidly, sitting back in her chair.

"Mineral water," Ann said.

"At least have a drink," Amy said when the waiter left. "I need one, and I wasn't even there."

Ann shook her head.

"What did you say to him?" Amy asked.

"I told him no, of course. Did you think I said yes?"

"Well, Annie, you do need the help, and you were desperately in love with him once upon a time. Not to mention that the man is beautiful and sexy and rich as Midas.''

''And plotting my destruction even as we speak.''

''What does that mean?''

''Why do you think he wants to marry me, Amy?'' Amy was silent.

''Can't you guess? You remember him, right? Did he ever strike you as the forgiving type?''

''No,'' Amy admitted.

''He wants revenge. He wants to have me in his house, legally bound to him, so he can torture me every day and make my life a purgatory. Got the picture now?''

''He said that to you?''

''Of course he didn't *say* that. One look at his face and I knew it. In Timmy's downfall he imagines he has the perfect vehicle to pay me back for what I did to him eleven years ago.''

''What he *thinks* you did to him.''

Ann shrugged.

''Well, didn't you tell him what actually happened?''

''I tried, but he wouldn't listen. He made up his mind when he was nineteen and nothing has changed it since. He was so prepared for the rich bitch to turn on him that when it happened there was only one possible explanation—the princess was unable to abandon the royal Talbot existence for a real life as his wife. I could present him with affidavits from archangels that tell a different story and they wouldn't mean a thing. He hates me, and he's been feeding that hatred for over a decade. In fact, I think it fueled his ambition, spurred on the desire to show me and the rest of the world that the half-breed kid from Hispaniola could make good."

Amy accepted her drink from the waiter and took a large sip from it as the waiter asked, "Will you ladies be having lunch?"

Amy nodded. "I'll have a Caesar salad with braised chicken and an iced tea. Ann?"

"Nothing for me," Ann said, and the waiter walked away.

"Please don't go on a hunger strike, that certainly won't help matters," Amy said sternly.

Ann looked across at her friend, who was always watching her weight and maintained her figure at great cost with starvation diets and gym fees, wishing she could summon up Amy's lusty appetite. If the slightest thing went wrong in Ann's life, she couldn't eat.

She had lost eight pounds in the last several weeks.

"What are you going to do?" Amy asked, fingering her perfectly coiffed and frosted hair.

"I'm going to find some way to get Tim out of jail that does not involve taking charity from Heath Bodine."

"I can give you about fifteen thousand right now," Amy offered, unbuttoning the jacket of her three-piece outfit, the style up-to-the-minute and very flattering. Amy was always the perfect advertisement for her profession.

"Thanks, Amy, that's very sweet, but—"

"I can get more if I break my father's trust," Amy added.

Amy's wealthy father had financed her education at the same private school Ann had attended, but since her parents' divorce, his money had been tied up for Amy until she was thirty. She couldn't touch it for two more years.

"Money isn't the only problem, Amy. The judge thinks Tim is a flight risk and wants to keep him locked up."

"How can Heath help you with that?"

"He intimated that some high-priced legal talent might convince the court otherwise."

"I see. One hand washes the other."

"Right. If somebody the judge knows suddenly shows up as Tim's counsel, things might work out very differently."

Amy stirred the ice in her drink. "I wish I could stay down here and help you, but I have to be in my office tomorrow morning. I'm catching a flight out tonight."

"It's all right, Amy. It's my problem and I'll deal with it."

"Forgive me for saying so, but you don't seem capable of dealing with anything right at the moment."

"Thanks a lot."

"It's the truth," Amy said as the waiter served her salad and left the check. "How much do you weigh these days?"

"Who knows? I avoid scales," Ann lied.

"So do I, but for a different reason. And have you been sleeping? You look exhausted."

"I've been taking transatlantic calls from lawyers at three o'clock in the morning and then staying up for the rest of the night wondering what to do about this awful mess. I'm sure Heath was thrilled to see me like this. He, of course, looks like he just came back from a month at a spa."

"Damn his eyes," Amy said, forking romaine lettuce into her mouth. "But he always was the juiciest thing on Lime Island. Remember him at nineteen? Luscious. But he could see only you."

"I'd rather not relive it, okay, Amy," Ann said softly.

"Yeah, right. Sorry. Listen, I was just thinking. I'm coming back to Largo at Christmas to see my mother, do you think you will still be here?"

"I hope not. I'd like to wrap this up quickly and return to New York as soon as I can."

"And you think Heath is just going to go away?" Amy asked, raising one brow inquiringly.

"I don't care what he does. He can't force me into anything, it's still a free country."

"Are you staying here at the inn?"

"Yes. The bank repossessed Tim's condo on the island and my parents' house was sold years ago. This seemed convenient to downtown and Caldwell's law office."

"You mean that nobody local has even called you and offered you a sandwich? Not any of your mother's friends?" Amy asked quietly, appalled.

Ann shrugged. "Maybe they don't know I'm here. I didn't exactly announce my return in ten-inch banner headlines. Even if they do know, I imagine they're all too embarrassed to talk to me. I mean, what would we discuss? My brother the felon, and his illegal activities? Quite a comedown from the country club."

"I still think it's terrible."

"Nothing creates distance like an impending indictment," Ann said dryly.

Amy glanced at her watch and then drained her Scotch. "Listen, sweetie, I hate to leave this wonderful food, but I have to go. I have to do some shopping at Burdine's, and then stop off at the Island Bank and see the trust officer, and—''

Ann held up her hand. ''Don't explain, I understand. I didn't exactly expect to be dropping this bomb about Heath, I thought handling Tim's crisis would be enough for one day.''

Amy rose and grabbed the check. ''Your mineral water is on me.'' She extracted a pen from her purse and scribbled on the back of a receipt. ''Here's a bunch of numbers where you can reach me. You already have my apartment where you can leave a message on the machine if I'm not there,'' Amy said.

Ann nodded.

''Call anytime. I mean it. I feel like a beast for rushing off like this, but if I'm not in my office tomorrow morning, heads will roll and mine will be first.'' She leaned over to kiss Ann on the cheek and then gave the thumbs-up sign as she began to weave her way between the tables on the restaurant terrace, her mind already on her errands.

Ann sat by herself for so long that the waiter finally returned and asked her if she wanted anything else.

''No, thanks, I'm fine,'' Ann said, emerging from her reverie. She rose to go to the reception desk and get her room key. As she was riding up in the elevator, she realized that she had lived on Lime Island for seventeen years but had never stayed in this hotel. The closest she had come to it was attending several parties in its ballroom. But in those days her life had consisted mainly of parties, here and at the Lime Country Club—a charmed existence that had not prepared her for the emotional desolation that followed.

The message light was blinking on her phone when she entered her room. Sighing, she sat on the edge of her bed and dialed the desk, hearing without surprise that Harold Caldwell wanted her to call him.

"Miss Talbot, I'm glad you were able to get back to me so quickly," the attorney said when she reached him.

"I'm sorry I didn't get a chance to sign the papers you had for me," Ann replied. "I'll come back to your office tomorrow."

"That will be fine, but that's not the reason I'm calling."

"Has something happened?" Ann asked anxiously. Something *else* she added silently.

"I'm afraid so."

Ann's heart sank at his tone. "Tell me."

"Your brother has been transferred to a hospital about ten miles from the county jail where he was being held pending disposition of his case," Caldwell said.

"Hospital?" Ann said faintly.

"Yes. It seems he got into an altercation with one of the other inmates and came out the worse for it."

"How bad?" Ann said quickly.

"He has a fractured skull and a broken leg."

Ann gasped, gripping the phone. "How could that happen? Don't they have guards in those places?"

"Of course they do, but fights among convicts are commonplace—they really can't be stopped completely."

"My brother is *not* a convict, Mr. Caldwell," Ann said tersely, on the verge of tears for the second time that day.

"Certainly not, it was just a figure of speech, please forgive me. I am so sorry to be giving you more bad news, but I thought you should know about this new development immediately."

Ann said nothing.

"What was the result of your conference with Mr. Bodine?" Caldwell asked, obviously hoping for a ray of light in this ocean of darkness.

"May I call you back tomorrow, Mr. Caldwell? I'll discuss it with you then."

"Certainly, but don't wait too long. If your brother has become a target in this particular jail, he could be in for more trouble once he is released from the hospital."

"Can't you have him transferred or something?"

"It's not as easy as it sounds, Miss Talbot. I would have to show cause . . ."

"A fractured skull isn't cause enough?" Ann asked, her voice rising.

"I will try. I just can't promise anything," the lawyer said. "I know this is a difficult time for you, but we have to address this whole situation quickly, not just the transfer, but the matter of Tim's bail. If I could get him released, we obviously wouldn't have to worry about the rest of it anymore."

"Work on it, and I'll call you first thing in the morning," Ann replied, and hung up the phone. Then she stretched out on the bed with her face down into the pillow for a long time.

When she finally stood, there was a determination in her movements that bespoke a renewed purpose.

She went into the adjoining bathroom and turned on the shower full force, waiting until the steam billowed out into the bedroom before shedding her clothes and stepping under the gushing, almost scalding water. She took a long, luxurious shower, letting the heat soak into her bones and the purifying steam clear her head. By the time she turned off the water and reached for the hotel robe hanging on the back of the bathroom door, she had made up her mind.

Ann went straight to the phone and dialed information, asking for the Miami number of Bimini Boat Works. When told by a sweet-voiced secretary that Mr. Bodine was not in his office, Ann left the message that she had called, along with her phone extension at the inn.

She was sitting in the armchair next to the phone ten minutes later when it rang.

"You called me?" Heath said without preliminary when she picked up the receiver and said hello.

Just the sound of his voice made her hands start to shake. "I'd like to get together and discuss the details of your offer," Ann said quietly.

"I'll meet you for dinner at the inn's restaurant tomorrow night at eight o'clock," he replied. He didn't ask why she had changed her mind so quickly. He didn't ask why she had changed her mind at all.

Obviously he didn't care.

"Fine," she said.

Ann heard a click as the line went dead. He had hung up without saying goodbye. Somehow, it seemed appropriate.

When you made a deal with the devil, common courtesy was probably de trop.

She sat back in the chair and for the first time since she'd returned to Florida she let her mind dwell on that fateful summer eleven years earlier, when she first met Heath. She had pushed the memories back for so long that when she finally opened the floodgate they all came rushing through, under pressure, drowning her in technicolor images of the past. She saw Heath as he had been; then as now, the most beautiful man she had ever seen....

Chapter 3

Eleven years earlier...

Ann pulled off her sunglasses and sat up in annoyance, looking around for the source of the noise. She had been up late at a dance the night before and was trying to take a nap, but someone was racing the motor of her father's powerboat. Every time she thought the grating sound had stopped, it would begin again, wearing on her nerves. She'd just been on the edge of sleep during a period of blessed silence when the engine roared to life once more.

Ann winced and sighed. The sound was drowning out the gentle lapping of the water against the bulkhead behind her. Ann fastened the straps of her bikini top and grabbed a towel from her deck chair, padding barefoot across the patio and the lawn and down to the dock that fronted the canal running behind her house. A thirty-two foot cabin cruiser and a twenty-foot speedboat were tied up there, the speed-boat with its engine racing. Ann stood on the dock, hands on hips, waiting for the din to subside. When it finally did she yelled "Hey!" and paused for a response.

There was none.

Muttering to herself, she climbed down into the front of the boat and walked around to the rear well, where a deeply tanned figure was bent over the engine housing, fiddling with a screwdriver.

"I'm talking to you," Ann said loudly.

The man turned to look up at her, and she froze under his stare, finally taking a step back and draping her towel self-consciously over her shoulders.

She felt as if he were undressing her with his eyes.

He was about six feet tall, his skin nut brown from the sun, his hair and brows and lashes blue-black, the color of anthracite. His face was arresting: wide amber eyes, a narrow nose, high cheekbones and a sculpted mouth with a thin upper lip and a full, cushioned lower one. His expression was not friendly as he looked her over, taking in her scanty bathing suit, bare feet and hair pinned up in a careless bun. He didn't look more than a few years older than Ann. She fingered a hanging tendril nervously as he said shortly, "What do you want?"

"I want you to stop making all this noise," Ann replied, her discomfiture making her sound equally abrupt.

"You from the house?" he said, jerking his head toward the lawn. He climbed out of the engine well and dropped the hatch.

"Yes."

"You giving me an order?"

Ann gazed back at him, unsure of how to reply. He was wearing cut-off jeans that frayed to a stop at his muscular thighs, with lace-up work boots and nothing else. Perspiration ran in rivulets down his arms and back and his hair was damp with it. He was lean, but not thin, his well-developed biceps flexing as he moved. A sprinkling of black chest hair spread over his flat nipples and disappeared in a narrow line below the waistband of his jeans. He had a flat, concave stomach, ridged and tight, and his limbs were traced with a laborer's prominent veins. His hands and the tip of his nose were smeared with engine grease.

Ann realized she was staring and looked away. "Wh-what do you mean?"

"You hired me. If you want me to stop, I'll stop."

"My father must have hired you. It's his boat."

The workman wiped his forehead with the back of his arm and then pulled a folded sheet of paper from the rear pocket of his jeans. "Henry Talbot?" he said.

"That's my father."

"I'm from Jensen's Marina. I have an order from Henry Talbot to tune up this engine—it's been misfiring. It can wait if the noise is bothering you too much. I'll come back."

He was looking at her with his cat's eyes, hands on hips, waiting for her response. Ann could only imagine her father's reaction if she caused a delay in the repair of his precious toy.

"No, go ahead. It's getting too hot out here anyway, I'll go inside." Ann walked to the front of the boat and then realized that he was following her. She stopped short and looked around at him. He hopped onto the dock in one graceful movement and then bent down, extending his hand to help her climb out of the boat. He saw that his fingers were covered with sticky engine fluid, so he wiped them on on his pants, then reached out to her again.

Ann slipped her hand into his and he pulled her up next to him. He was so strong that she seemed to fly through the air and land on the dock with no effort at all on her part.

"Thanks," she said, looking up into his face.

"No problem, Princess," he said, and smiled.

His teeth were very white against his dark face, the incisors slightly crooked. A silence grew between them as they stood on the dock, immobile, their eyes locked.

Luisa appeared in the kitchen doorway and called, "Miss Ann, your mother wants to speak to you."

Ann tore her eyes away from her companion and said, "All right, Luisa, I'm coming in now."

"So long, Princess," he said, and hopped down into the boat. He disappeared around the curve of the bow as she looked after him, then Ann turned reluctantly toward the house.

Luisa was making lunch as Ann came inside, closing the sliding-glass door behind her to contain the conditioned air. Luisa nodded toward the hall and Ann went down to her mother's room.

"Mom?" she said, outside her parents' door.

"Come in," her mother called.

Ann walked into the dressing room, where her mother was stepping into a pair of pumps.

"Hi, honey. I just wanted to let you know that I'll be having lunch at the club. I've already told Luisa to save something for your father whenever he wanders in from his golf game, so just be a good girl and eat whatever she gives you, okay? And remember, those carpet people are coming, so stay out of their way and let them work. Your father has been griping about the stains in his den for the last three months. What are your plans for the afternoon?'' Margaret Talbot's cool, aristocratic tones, still retaining a hint of New England, floated toward Ann as her mother clipped on a pair of earrings.

"I thought I'd just hang around here, maybe take a swim. Amy is coming over tonight."

"All right, sweetie, have fun. It's so nice to have you home again. And remember, we're going shopping tomorrow on the big island." Her mother came over to her and kissed her cheek.

"Okay."

"See you at dinner. Bye-bye." Margaret picked up her purse and tennis racket, grabbing her carryall and waving to her daughter as she left the bedroom.

"'Bye." Ann followed her mother into the hall, returning to the kitchen to find Luisa pouring out a glass of iced lemonade. Several oatmeal and raisin cookies and a folded napkin sat beside it on a ceramic tray.

"Is that my lunch?" Ann asked.

"Of course not, your mother would have a fit," Luisa replied crisply.

"It's for that boy working on the boat, isn't it?" Ann said, snatching a cookie.

"So?"

"I'll take it out to him."

"You will not," Luisa said firmly.

"Why not?"

"Your father wouldn't want you talking to that boy," Luisa replied, picking up the tray herself.

"What's wrong, is he a criminal or something?" Ann asked around a mouthful of oatmeal, intrigued.

Luisa didn't answer, merely walked toward the back patio, the tray in her hands.

"So then why is it okay for you to talk to him, Luisa?" Ann inquired logically, abandoning the remains of the cookie on the kitchen table.

The front doorbell rang.

"I think you'd better get that," Ann said to Luisa, deftly taking the tray from the older woman's hands.

"You can answer it," Luisa said.

"No, I can't. It's the carpet cleaners, I can see the van through the window. You have to talk to them."

Luisa sighed and turned around as Ann slipped through the patio doors, balancing the tray with one hand as she moved the slider closed with the other.

Ann walked carefully over the back lawn toward the boat as the ice clinked in the tall glass. She was almost to the boat when she heard a yelp and a curse, followed by frantic rummaging sounds. She put the tray down on the lawn and ran the rest of the way, jumping down from the dock and peering into the engine well.

The workman was sitting cross-legged on the deck, wrapping a filthy towel around his hand as blood gushed from his thumb.

"Oh, my God," Ann said, running to his side. "What on earth did you do?"

"I was trimming the fuel line when the knife slipped," he replied tersely, wadding the dingy terry cloth against his hand. It was rapidly turning red.

"That's really bleeding badly, you have to get to the hospital," Ann said. "Let me just run inside and get my car keys and I'll take you there."

"No way," he replied. "My truck is parked out by the road, I can drive."

"You can't drive with your hand like that, especially a manual transmission," Ann said, already turning for the house. She didn't wait for him to answer, but sprinted back inside, grabbing her purse from her dresser and pulling a pair of shorts on over her bikini bottoms. She paused to slip into her sandals as Luisa came after her and asked, "Where do you think you're going? Lunch is almost ready."

"The boy working on the boat hurt his hand badly, I'm taking him to Palm Hospital," Ann replied, running for the side door leading to the garage.

"You can't drive him all the way to the hospital!" Luisa called anxiously, scuttling after her charge. "Let one of the carpet cleaners take him."

"Don't be ridiculous," Ann said to Luisa over her shoulder, jumping into her car and pressing the release for the garage door, which began to ascend automatically behind them. "They have a schedule to keep and they're already unraveling the hose from the van. And you know what my father will say if his rug isn't cleaned on time. I'm doing nothing, I can take him. Now get out of the way so I can back up the car, okay?"

Luisa moved reluctantly, her expression unhappy, as Ann backed the car down the long drive leading to the street. Once there she saw that the workman was trying to do a U-turn in his ancient truck, operating the controls with his injured hand.

Ann zoomed in front of him, blocking his truck with her car. She got out, leaving her door open as she walked over to him and looked up inquiringly into the cab.

"Get out of my way," he said tightly, not even pausing to glance at her.

"Having a little trouble?" she asked mildly.

"I'll make it," he replied shortly.

"Sure you will, if you can manage to drive that Stone Age truck with your mangled hand and don't pass out from loss of blood along the way."

"Not all of us can afford a new sports car every year, Miss Talbot," he said irritably. He threw the truck into reverse awkwardly and it lurched and died. He closed his eyes.

"Very good—looks like you're stuck. Now will you stop being such a macho idiot and let me drive you to the hospital?"

He said nothing, his conflicted expression indicating the struggle between his overwhelming desire to handle the situation himself and his realization that she was right. Logic finally won and he put the truck into neutral and let it roll to the side of the road. Then he jumped down from the cab and said tersely, "I'm going to bleed all over your fancy leather upholstery."

"Why don't you let me worry about that?" Ann replied, getting back behind the wheel of her car as he slid into the front seat on the passenger side, trying futilely to rewrap the already sopping towel around his wound.

"Use this," she said, grabbing a sweater from her back seat and handing it to him.

"Isn't this yours?" he said, accepting the garment with his good hand.

"I have others," she said shortly.

He shot her an unreadable glance and then did as she said, dropping the towel on the floor and substituting her pullover for it. He cradled the injured hand in his lap and sat bolt upright, looking out the window as Ann drove.

"Why don't you sit back and relax?" she said to him. "I'm not going to bite you."

He obeyed, letting his shoulders touch the seat and closing his eyes. He looked pale beneath his tan and seemed drained. The loss of blood, or the shock of the accident, must have been affecting him.

"You should hold your hand upright and put pressure on the cut," Ann said. "It will slow the bleeding."

"Who are you, Florence Nightingale?"

"I had a first-aid course in school."

"Stop telling me what to do, okay?"

Ann shrugged. "Okay. I'm only trying to help."

Out of the corner of her eye Ann saw him lift the injured hand with the good one and press his opposing thumb over the cut.

She smiled to herself and kept on driving.

The trip to the hospital over the causeway to Big Palm Island took only ten minutes, but it seemed longer. When they reached the emergency room entrance he bolted out the door of her car as soon as it stopped moving.

"Hey, wait for me!" Ann called, throwing the gearshift into park and grabbing her keys from the ignition. By the time she got inside he was already registering with the clerk.

"Insurance?" the clerk said.

He shook his head.

"You have no insurance?" the clerk asked.

"That's right."

"I will pay cash for it," Ann said, producing her wallet.

He turned around and glared at her. "You're not paying for this with your old man's money!" he said in a fierce undertone.

"They might not take you otherwise."

He snatched the wallet from her hand and tossed it into a nearby trash can.

"You two kids want to take this outside?" the clerk said in a bored tone, pencil poised above the admitting form.

"I'll pay cash," he said firmly as Ann rooted in the trash for her wallet.

"Fine," the clerk said. "Fill in the bottom part of this form and then see the triage nurse."

He took the clipboard with his good hand and sat in one of the plastic chairs lined up in the emergency room. Ann, wallet secured, sat next to him.

"Look, you did me a favor and brought me here, now you can go," he said to her.

She looked back at him blankly.

"Thank you," he added shortly.

Ann didn't move.

He sighed and began to fill out the form, holding the clipboard awkwardly on his lap.

"You're getting bloodstains on that paper," Ann said.

He ignored her.

"You're putting the information in the wrong section," Ann noted pointedly, and he turned to her abruptly, dropping the clipboard on the floor. He groaned.

"Why don't you let me do it?" Ann suggested as she retrieved the board for him. "Just dictate and I'll write. You'll bleed to death before they see you at this rate."

"I can do it myself!" he said as her sweater slipped off his hand and a fresh smear of blood stained his pants.

Ann scribbled the date and time in the correct square and said, "Name?"

He closed his eyes in extreme forbearance, waited a beat and then said resignedly, "Heath Bodine."

"Last name spelling?"

He spelled it.

"Address?"

He gave a Port Lisbon address unfamiliar to her.

"Age?"

In the course of the exercise, she found out that he was a nineteen-year-old male and worked full-time at Jensen's Marina. Her reaction was disappointment. The only thing she hadn't known before was his age and she didn't learn any new information.

He turned in the form and was called by the triage nurse, who determined that he could wait his turn among the senior citizens, the toddler with a fever, and the plumber who had caught his hand in a pipe, all currently sitting in the reception area. He returned to his seat and stared straight ahead as Ann said, "Heath?"

He looked at her.

"Why are you trying so hard to get rid of me?"

"There's nothing more for you to do."

"I'd like to wait and make sure that you're all right."

"I'm all right, or the triage nurse would have sent me in ahead of the others. The cut's hardly bleeding anymore, you can see that. You can go."

She held his gaze with hers, feeling his cat's eyes penetrating to her very soul. She felt like she was drowning in them.

"Humor me, okay?" she said softly.

His lips relaxed slowly into the trace of a smile.

"Okay," he said.

They sat in companionable silence for another fifteen minutes. Toward the end of the wait, Ann got up from her seat and purchased a can of orange juice from a nearby vending machine. She took a sip and then handed it to him.

"What's this?" he said.

"An atomic bomb," she answered.

He shot her a sidelong glance.

"Juice to help your system replenish the blood you've lost," Ann said.

"Another souvenir of your first-aid course?" he said.

"Haven't you ever donated blood?" Ann asked. "They always give you juice and cookies."

"Good works are not high on my list of activities," he replied dryly. "So, where are my cookies?"

"I'm working under makeshift conditions here. Juice is the best I can do."

An emergency room nurse in surgical greens came through the admitting door and called Heath's name.

"Courage!" Ann whispered as he got up, and he looked back at her, obviously suppressing a grin.

When he returned a short time later, he had four stitches in his hand and a prescription for antibiotics. He didn't volunteer what he had done about the bill and Ann didn't ask.

"Thanks a lot for your help," he said, grimacing down at the bandage on his palm. "I can get home from here."

"I'll drive you."

He stared at her.

"Don't give me an argument, Heath. You have no transportation and I'm standing right here with a fully functioning car waiting outside that entrance."

He shrugged and followed her through the glass doors to the parking lot. They got into the car and he sat with his long legs stretched out, speaking only to give her directions. When he told her to stop, she looked around in bewilderment. They were at an intersection with railroad tracks on one side and a series of bars on the other.

"There are no houses here," she said.

"That's right."

"But where is yours?"

"I can walk."

"Don't be ridiculous. I'll drop you off at the door."

He was already out of the car. He leaned back in through his open window and said, "Thanks for what you did, Princess. I really do appreciate it."

Ann watched in amazement as he walked off down the street. Short of chasing him down with the car, she had to let him go.

He obviously didn't want her to see where he lived.

Ann made a U-turn in the middle of the street and went back the way she had come.

* * *

Luisa was waiting for Ann in the front hall of the Talbot house when she returned.

"What happened? Are you all right?"

"Of course I'm all right, Luisa. What's the matter with you? I took Heath to the hospital, they stitched up his hand, and I drove him home. End of story."

"You drove him home?"

"Well, to the intersection at Railroad Avenue. He wouldn't let me go any farther. Where does he live, anyway?"

"Never mind about that, just sit down and eat your lunch. I've reheated the soup."

"I don't want any lunch, Luisa. I want you to tell me why you're so twitchy about that guy. Did he just bust out of the county jail or something?"

"Your father would not consider him suitable company," Luisa said expressionlessly.

"Why, because he lives in Hispaniola? So do you."

"All poor people are not the same," Luisa said firmly. "My family may not have much money, but we are always respectable. We work hard, we take care of our children, and we don't accept welfare." Her tone was disdainful.

"And Heath's family?"

Luisa set a bowl of soup on the kitchen table and pointed to a chair. "Sit," she said.

Ann sat. "If I eat my porridge like a good little bear, will you tell me?"

"It's none of your business. Why are you so interested in that boy's background?"

"I'm just curious, that's all."

"You're curious about too much that doesn't concern you, young lady."

"That's because nobody ever tells me anything." Ann lifted a spoonful of steaming vegetable soup to her mouth and swallowed it ostentatiously. "It's too hot for soup, anyway, whose idea was this?" she said peevishly.

"Your mother wants you to have a balanced diet."

"She's probably eating potato chips and onion dip for lunch at the club," Ann muttered. "With chocolate turtles for dessert."

"Your mother is an adult."

"So am I. In six months, anyway, according to the State of Florida."

"Until then, you'll eat your soup."

Ann peered over at the housekeeper, who was now folding dish towels. "What happened to the truck Heath left here earlier?" Ann asked. "I didn't see it when I drove in just now."

"I called the marina and they sent someone to pick it up," Luisa replied.

Ann absorbed the information in silence. Luisa hadn't wanted Heath to return for it.

"He's going to come back to fix the engine on the speedboat," Ann said. "He wasn't done with it."

"The two men who came here for the truck fixed the engine," Luisa said shortly. "The job is finished."

Ann dipped her spoon in and out of her soup thoughtfully. "If you dislike Heath so much, why were you fixing him a snack today, before he was hurt?"

"I don't dislike him. You can't blame a child for his parents," Luisa replied cryptically, and stalked off to the linen closet with the stack of towels.

Ann pushed the soup bowl away and folded her arms on the table, twirling a strand of her hair around her finger thoughtfully.

One way or another, she was going to find out more about Heath Bodine.

Amy Horton propped one leg up on a pillow and inspected her bare toenails. "What do you think, *amiga mia?* Papaya Passion or Suncoral Kiss?"

"Suncoral Kiss," Ann replied, handing her friend the bottle of bright nail polish. She tiptoed to the door of her room and opened it a crack, making sure her parents were still having after-dinner coffee in the den. Then she turned back to Amy, who was sprawled on the double bed, carefully dabbing coral-colored goo onto the nail of her right big toe.

"Do you know a guy from the island, a couple of years older than us, named Bodine?" she asked Amy.

Amy's brush stopped moving as she looked up suddenly and said, "Heath Bodine?"

"Yeah."

"Of course I know him. He's only the cutest guy on Lime Island. He graduated from Palm High with my cousin Carol. She was crazy about him but he would never give her the time of day."

"Amy, your cousin Carol is crazy about everybody—that doesn't mean very much."

"Why do you ask?"

"I met him today."

"You met Heath Bodine?" Ann now had Amy's undivided attention. "Where?"

"Right here. He came to fix my father's boat and cut himself. I took him to the hospital."

Amy put the bottle of polish aside and sat up eagerly. "Is he as gorgeous as Carol says? I've never seen him."

"He's pretty adorable," Ann admitted. "What I can't understand is why Luisa was trying to keep me away from him. She did everything but tie me to a chair."

"Well, she's from Hispaniola, too, she probably knows his story," Amy replied.

"What *is* his story, for heaven's sake? Luisa wouldn't tell me a thing."

"I think Carol said his father is a drunk and the mother abandoned the family. Before she left she was kind of... promiscuous, I guess. That's what Carol says, anyway. I know his older sister was on drugs and went to Miami to work the streets to support her habit. She died of an overdose a couple of years ago."

"How awful," Ann murmured.

"I know you don't think Carol is a reliable source, but most of that is true. I've heard her parents talking about it."

Carol's parents represented the less affluent branch of the Horton family, which was why Carol had attended the local public high school with Heath and not Winfield Academy with Amy and Ann. Carol was currently staying up in North Carolina taking a summer course in journalism at Chapel Hill.

"I don't like the look on your face, Talbot," Amy added. "What are you going to do?"

"I don't know."

"Did he say he would call you or anything?"

"No."

"Did he act interested?"

"Not really. He kept trying to get rid of me, but still, there was a look in his eye...."

"That certainly clears it up," Amy said dryly. "You do realize that if you go after this guy your father will have a stroke and a coronary at the same time. His idea of the perfect date for you is Alan Michael Witherspoon." She picked up the bottle of polish again and resumed her task.

Ann made a retching sound and dropped into the chair by her bedroom window. "Alan Witherspoon still wears braces and has zits on the back of his neck."

"His father has forty million dollars, and someday Alan will, too," Amy replied sagely.

"He has the most beautiful almond-shaped eyes, the color of sherry, and these silky black hairs on the backs of his hands...." Ann said dreamily.

"Alan Witherspoon?" Amy inquired teasingly.

"No, dummy, Heath Bodine. And the longest eyelashes, and the sexiest smile...."

"I see you took a complete inventory. Look, you don't have to convince me. Carol would have strolled stark naked down Prospect Boulevard if she thought it would make that guy give her a second glance. I'm just telling you that I can guess why Luisa was acting so weird. Your father probably didn't know who the marina was going to send to your house, and when Luisa saw Heath she decided that it was her duty to discourage your attraction to him." Amy daintily daubed a toenail, cleaning its edge with her pinkie.

"She didn't know I was attracted to him."

"From what I've heard, anyone with the appropriate estrogen levels would be attracted to him. Luisa isn't stupid. She figured if you got a look at each other, sparks might fly—and she was right." Amy put the cap on the bottle of polish and set it on Ann's dresser, then inspected her foot admiringly.

"Yeah, well, I'll probably never see him again. The marina sent somebody else to finish the job on my father's boat and from Heath's attitude I doubt if he'll be inviting me over to his house for tea anytime soon."

There was a knock at Ann's door. It opened and Mrs. Talbot stuck her head into the room.

"Ice cream, ladies," she said. "Come on out to the table if you want some."

Both girls rose, Amy walking on her heels to protect the drying polish, and Ann sent Amy a silencing glance.

"How did you do in the tennis round-robin today, Mrs. Talbot?" Amy asked innocently as they walked down the hall to the kitchen.

Chapter 4

The next morning Ann's father was at his office, her mother was at a Daughters of the American Revolution meeting, and Luisa was at the market doing the grocery shopping. Ann was deep into the adventures of a Victorian Gothic heroine in the Yorkshire dales when the doorbell rang. Ann padded barefoot over to the front hall to answer it, saving her place in her book with her finger.

Heath Bodine stood on the front portico, Ann's sweater in his hands.

"Hi," he said. "Okay if I come in?"

Ann's heart began to beat faster the moment she saw him. He was wearing tan chino pants with a crisp navy polo shirt that flattered his dark coloring. She stood aside and let him walk past her into the house.

"How's your hand?" she asked.

"It's all right. They did a good job sewing it up at

the hospital, I guess." He handed her the sweater, now spotless. "I brought this back for you."

"You got the bloodstains out!" Ann said, marveling.

He smiled wryly. "I've been working at the marina for five years now. Stain removal is my life."

Ann laughed.

"Would you like a cup of coffee or something? There's nobody home but me," Ann said, leading the way into the living room of the house.

"I know. I stayed across the street until I saw everybody else leave."

Ann looked at him inquiringly.

"I wanted to talk to you alone."

Ann waited, her mouth going dry.

"I guess Luisa told you all about me," he said flatly, his gaze expectant.

Ann shook her head.

"Yeah, she got rid of the truck so I wouldn't have to come back to your house. That's why I'm here."

"What do you mean?"

"I don't appreciate being driven away like a thief," Heath said darkly.

"Luisa didn't mean it like that."

"Oh, no?" he said, holding her eyes steadily with his own, his posture defiant.

Ann looked away from him.

"There's another reason I came," he added.

"Yes?" Ann said.

"It was a nice thing you did for me, and I know I wasn't acting very grateful."

"Don't worry about it, I understand. You were in pain, and worried about your hand...."

"That wasn't it," he said.

Ann stopped.

"People like you look down on people like me, and I didn't want to be indebted to any snob."

"I'm not a snob, Heath."

"I realized that after I got home and thought about it. I guess I just reacted instinctively, and I'm sorry."

He extended his hand, and she took it. His palm was callused and warm.

The telephone rang and they both jumped, as if caught in a stolen embrace.

"Just let me answer that," Ann said hastily, "and I'll be right back."

When she got to the phone it was her father, calling from work. That was odd enough in itself to make her wonder what was going on. Henry Talbot's business was his life, and when he left the house in the morning it was usually as if he had disappeared into a parallel universe until he returned in the evening.

"I just wanted to let you know that there's a dance at the Heron Club this Friday night and Dan Witherspoon asked me if you and Alan Michael would like to attend," Henry said.

Ann saw the fine hand of Luisa in this development. The housekeeper had obviously told Henry about the incident with Heath, and Henry's response was to provide his daughter with what he considered a more appropriate alternative.

Ann's grip tightened on the receiver. She had spent exactly two hours with Heath Bodine, most of it in an intensely romantic hospital emergency room, and her father was behaving as if she had been discovered in a motel bed with him.

"Mr. Witherspoon is now arranging Alan's dates?" Ann said to her father.

"Don't be ridiculous," Henry Talbot replied testily. "He just thought it would be a nice idea if we could all go together."

"Well, I'm sorry, you're going to have to disappoint Mr. Witherspoon. I have plans for Friday."

"What are you doing?"

"Amy and I are going over to Big Palm Island for an Aerosmith concert."

"Can't you postpone that?"

"Dad, they're playing one night before going on to Miami. We've had the tickets for three months."

Henry sighed dramatically. "All right, we'll arrange something for the future then."

Over my cooling carcass, Ann thought. Aloud she asked, "Is that all, Daddy?"

"I suppose so. Tell your mother I'll be home at seven-fifteen. Goodbye."

"'Bye." Ann hung up the phone and walked back into the living room—to discover that Heath was gone.

"What do you mean, he left?" Amy said as they drove over the causeway to Big Palm on Friday night.

"Just what I said. I went into the kitchen to get the phone and when I came back he was gone."

"That's odd."

"Not to mention rude."

"I don't think he was being rude," Amy said thoughtfully, turning down the radio.

"What would you call it?"

"He probably had to work up his nerve to come and see you, and then when you left he felt uncertain about it. Maybe he thought you were trying to get rid of him."

"He heard the phone ringing in the kitchen, Amy. It wasn't a magic trick."

"But you did stay talking on the phone for several minutes, right?"

"It was my father, Amy. You know what he's like."

"Heath doesn't know that. He may have thought you seized the opportunity to escape."

"That's stupid, Amy, why would I do that? He was only returning my sweater."

Amy turned to look at her in amazement. "You're the one who's stupid, Annie. He could have mailed the sweater to you. He wanted to see you again and the sweater was an excuse."

"You really think so?"

Amy rolled her eyes. "You've spent too much time in an all-girls' school, sweetie."

"You've been going to the same school."

"But I sneak out every weekend to drive to Far Hills Community College to party while you stay in our room and read Victoria Holt novels and watch old movies. Trust me, I know about these things. He's hooked."

"I'd like to see him again," Ann said softly.

"Then do it," Amy said firmly.

"What do you mean?"

"Tonight is the perfect opportunity. Your parents think you're at the concert with me. I'll drop you off at Jensen's Marina."

"I can't do that!" Ann said, aghast.

"Why not?"

"It's so... forward."

"What is this, 1959? Is Donna Reed at your house, giving advice in a shirtwaist dress, high heels and pearls? You want him, go for it."

"I don't even know if he's working tonight."

"From what I hear, he's always there. I don't think home is too much fun. But we can make sure. Let's pull over and call him."

Ann stared at her in horror.

"I won't say who it is, I'll just ask for him and see if he's there, okay?" Amy said, shrugging innocently.

Ann hesitated.

"Come on, come on—no guts, no glory." Amy pulled into a driveway and turned her car around, heading back toward Lime Island.

"What if he is there? Are you going on to the concert by yourself?"

"Are you kidding? Gloria Stansfield has been bugging me for weeks to sell her my ticket, she'll take yours in a second. I know for a fact she's home tonight, I just talked to her this morning. I can pick her up after I drop you off at Jensen's."

"Got it all figured out, haven't you?"

"Yup," Amy said smugly, and grinned.

She guided her red Camaro into the Jiffy Stop strip mall and stopped the car in front of the pay phone. "Well?" she said as she put the car in park.

"All right. Should I call?"

Amy shook her head. "He might recognize your voice if he comes to the phone or answers it himself. This way, if I call and then you chicken out, he won't be the wiser."

Ann watched as Amy got out of the car and went to the phone. She had to hand it to her more sophisticated friend; Amy was a whiz at this stuff.

She saw Amy's lips moving and then waited what seemed like an eternity before Amy flashed her the thumbs-up sign and nodded emphatically.

Ann felt her heart lurch. She had been half hoping that Heath wouldn't be there. As much as she wanted to see him again, the thought of actually confronting him made her go weak in the knees.

What if he told her to get lost?

Amy scampered back to the car and chortled "Bingo" as she pulled open the door. She started the engine and the car shot out into the street, its tires kicking up sprays of gravel in her eagerness to get back onto the road.

"What took you so long?" Ann demanded, gnawing on her thumbnail.

"I had to get the number of the marina from information first. I didn't exactly have it memorized, you know."

"What did he say?"

"I didn't talk to him. When somebody answered I just asked her for Heath Bodine, and when she went to get him, I hung up the phone. But we know he's there."

"For how long?"

"Probably until the place closes at nine."

"But what if he leaves early? What if he goes out on a job and isn't there when I arrive?"

Amy looked over at her in exasperation. "Then take a cab back home. Luisa's gone for the day and your parents are out, anyway, they'll never know the difference."

"I only have ten dollars."

Amy picked up her purse from the car's console with her free hand and thrust it into Ann's lap.

"There's fifty in my wallet, take half. That'll be more than enough, even if the cabbie takes you home by way of Santiago. Anything else, Nervous Nellie?"

"I'm not dressed right."

"Oh, for heaven's sake, Annie. You're driving me nuts. You look perfectly fine."

"This blouse is old."

"It brings out the color of your eyes."

"My hair is frizzy."

"Sweetie, your hair would not frizz in the jungles of equatorial Africa. It looks the way it always does, sensational."

"I have a zit on my forehead."

Amy slowed the car and pulled onto the shoulder of the road. She put the car in neutral and looked over at her friend.

"We are three minutes from the marina. If you don't want to go through with this, say so now and we'll forget it, all right?"

Ann bit her lip. "I want to do it. I'm just... scared."

"Scared of him?"

"A little. He's so big and strong and, I don't know, masculine. And he must have a reputation, or else why would my father and Luisa be freaking out just because I talked to him?"

"Hold me back," Amy said, sighing. "If he were interested in me I would *live* at Jensen's Marina."

"Okay. Let's go."

The rest of the trip was conducted in silence. The marina was lit up as dusk was just falling, and through the glass walls of the showroom Ann could see the new boats up on blocks for display to potential buyers. The docks where the tenant boats bobbed at anchor led off to the water on the right; the repair garage was on the left.

"How are you doing?" Amy asked as she pulled to a stop at the entrance to the garage.

"I'm a wreck. My hands are like ice."

"Go for it. Good luck."

Ann got out of the car. Amy pulled away so fast that Ann knew Amy was not giving her a chance to change her mind.

Ann walked slowly inside the garage, where several boats were disassembled on the stained cement floor and the smell of oil and diesel fuel was overpowering. A middle-aged man with red hair, wearing a rugby shirt, looked up from a ledger at a desk by the door.

"Help you?" he said.

"Yes, I'm, uh, looking for Heath Bodine."

"He's out back with Joan. Want me to get him for you?""

Ann almost said no, but the man was already moving away. She stood shifting her weight nervously, wondering who Joan was, until she heard the sound of footsteps and saw Heath walking toward her.

He was wearing ripped and faded jeans with a sleeveless army surplus T-shirt and wiping his hands on a greasy rag. He stopped short when he saw her.

"What are you doing here?" he asked.

Ann stared at his unsmiling face, the hard lines of his mouth, and her nerve failed her.

"I'm sorry, I shouldn't have come," she muttered, bolting for the exit.

He ran in front of her and blocked her path. "Don't go," he said. "I was just surprised, I didn't expect to see you."

Ann looked back at him in mute appeal.

The redhead returned to his desk and examined the ledger again, humming under his breath.

"Joe, okay for me to use the office for a few minutes?" Heath said to him.

"Sure, kid. It's empty."

Heath jerked his head toward a cubicle with a door at their left, and Ann followed him into it. Once inside Heath turned to Ann and looked at her inquiringly.

"I don't know what I'm doing here," she said miserably. "I just wanted to see you again."

He gazed at her for a long moment and then walked past her to lock the door. When he turned back to her, his face was unguarded and vulnerable.

He opened his arms and she ran into them.

"It's all right, Princess," he said into her hair as she closed her eyes and relaxed into his embrace, reveling in the hard feel of his arms around her and the support of his shoulder under her cheek. "I feel the same way, I just wasn't sure if you did."

"I did. I do. I hadn't planned to leave you the other day when the phone rang, and when I came back and you were gone—"

"Don't explain," he said, interrupting her, and she felt the rumble of his voice under her ear. "It doesn't matter. You're here with me now, and that's what counts."

He held her off at arm's length to look down into her face, and then laughed.

"I'm getting you all dirty," he said.

She threw her arms around his neck again. "I don't care. Hold me again."

He obeyed, crushing her to him, and she felt his lips in her hair. When they moved down to her cheek, she lifted her mouth eagerly for his kiss.

It left her breathless, eager for more. He knew what he was doing; this was not the shy, tentative kiss of an inexperienced adolescent but the mature embrace of a man. She clung to him, her lips opening to admit his probing tongue, pressing herself against his lean body until she could feel his unmistakable reaction. It didn't alarm her, only made her hungry for more.

There was a knock at the door. "Hey, kid, I need to get in there for the day's receipts," a male voice said.

Heath pulled Ann's arms from around his neck and took a step back.

"We can't do this here," he said breathlessly. "Can you meet me when I get off work at nine?"

Ann nodded, her heart still pounding.

"I have my bike out back. We'll take a ride, okay?"

"Okay."

He moved to unlock the door. "And whatever you've heard about me or my family," he said, "don't be afraid. I'd never do anything to hurt you."

"I'm not afraid," she said, and suddenly she wasn't.

The door opened and the redhead came into the room, shooting Heath an amused glance.

"I'll see you later, okay?" Heath said to Ann, careful not to look at her.

"Later," she echoed, and walked out of the office and through the garage, not seeing a thing.

She waited until she was outside the doors before she jumped for joy.

The hour and a half until Heath got off work seemed to last a decade. Ann went to a sandwich shop down the block from the marina. She sat there nursing several sodas and staring uncomprehendingly at a newspaper until it was time to walk back to Jensen's. When she got there, the redhead was locking the doors of the garage with a woman standing at his side. He grinned at Ann and said, "Heath will be right out, miss."

Ann nodded.

Heath emerged from the office door, a gray, hooded sweatshirt tied around his waist. He smiled when he saw her and called out to the others, "G'night, Joe. G'night, Joanie."

The woman waved as the couple climbed into a van and the man started the motor.

"Joe and Joanie Jensen, sounds like a British comedy team," Ann said to Heath as he joined her.

"Yeah, I know, but they've been good to me. Joe took me on when I was just a sophomore in high school, didn't even have working papers, didn't know a thing. I've been here ever since." He took her hand as naturally as he had kissed her and led her around to the side of the building.

"Are you the only ones who work at night?"

"Actually, the place closes at six. They own the marina, so they're here after hours to do paperwork and bookkeeping, stuff like that. I come in some nights to finish whatever repairs they didn't get to during the day, and sort of clean up, you know?"

Ann nodded. She didn't even care what he was saying, his presence was so overwhelming. He stopped short in front of a huge Harley-Davidson chained to a cement post and said, "You ever been on one of these?"

Ann shook her head.

"I didn't think so," he said dryly. "Not exactly the mode of transportation favored by the country-club set, is it?"

Ann surveyed the motorcycle warily.

"We can just take a walk if you'd rather not get on it," he said, responding to her expression.

"No, it's all right. I want to try it. What do I do?"

"Just climb on behind me and hang on tight to my waist," he replied.

"I think I can do that," Ann said, blushing.

"Yeah, I'll bet you can," he replied, laughing. He released the chain and then sat on the bike, kicking it into life. Then he unsnapped a helmet from the crossbar and handed it to her.

"Put this on," he said to her.

"Where's yours?"

"That *is* mine. I wasn't expecting company. I'll get another one for you tomorrow. Come on aboard." He held out his hand and she took it confidently.

Ann felt a glow as she climbed onto the bike and wrapped her arms around Heath's waist. He was getting her a helmet. There would be more times like this.

"Okay back there?" he said, turning his head.

"Fine."

"Where to?"

"I don't care," Ann said, and she didn't.

They roared off down the incline from the marina to the street, and when Heath reached the road he opened up the bike, traveling at a rate of speed that made the wind whistle in Ann's ears and the night-time scenery merge into a blur. She leaned forward and put her head against the back of Heath's shoulder, closing her eyes and just enjoying the sensation of his warm, muscular body under her hands. When she finally felt the bike slow down she was almost sorry, raising her head to see that Heath was pulling into a clearing above the bay. They were on a height looking out toward the causeway bridge, which twinkled with strings of lights in the warm and fragrant darkness.

"It's so pretty," Ann said as he helped her off the bike. "How did you know about this spot? I've lived on Lime Island all my life and have never been here."

"I drive around a lot," he answered shortly. He untied the sweatshirt from his waist and spread it on the ground for her to sit upon in comfort. The innate gallantry of the gesture pleased her, and she sat with great ceremony, curling her legs under her.

"Where are we?" Ann asked.

"The hills above Port Lisbon. That's the commercial dock area down below, where you see the boats." He lay back on the grass and folded his hands behind his head, staring up at the stars. She could just see the white bandage near his thumb, smaller now. He had replaced the gauze pack from the hospital with a square of white tape.

Ann waited for him to speak, certain that he would, but curiously not anxious to rush him. Normally she was one of those people who charged in to fill the gap when a silence fell, but already she knew that with Heath, the situation was different.

He was not a talker.

He sat up suddenly and she could tell that he was looking at her, even though all she could see in the dim and filtered moonlight was his clean profile.

"Princess, I have to tell you the truth here," he said quietly. "I don't want to scare you, but I've never felt like this before, and I want to make sure you feel the same before this goes any further."

Ann held her breath, listening.

"Ever since we met on your father's boat, I've felt so drawn to you... like I have to be with you. Obviously I was fighting it the first day—I didn't want to make a fool of myself. It was happening so fast, so strong, and I know I have nothing to offer somebody like you."

"That isn't true," Ann protested. He held up his hand to stop her.

"Let me finish. When you came to see me tonight, I realized that you must be feeling the same thing."

"I am," Ann said softly.

"Okay. Then you should know about me. You're going to hear things from people—Lime Island is small and Port Lisbon is even smaller. Even though you didn't go to school here, you're going to be around all summer and Luisa Sanchez, who lives two blocks away from me, works in your house. I want you to know the facts."

"All right."

He sighed and stared off into the distance. "My father is the town drunk. He hasn't worked at all in about ten years, lives off welfare and has a buzz on by about eleven in the morning. In the afternoon he passes out on the sofa and gets up to stagger around a few hours in the evening before crashing into bed. Or in a chair, or on the floor. Whatever's handy.''

Ann said nothing.

''His daddy was a full-blooded Seminole, and he says it's the Indian blood in him that makes him drink, but I think he's just a lazy bastard who likes to lap up the sauce. As for my mother, she took off when I was nine, about the time my father really started to go downhill. I have no idea if his decline was the cause or the result of her leaving. We don't know where she is, and I don't care. Before she left she was an embarrassment, anyway, the *friendly* type, if you get my drift. She was especially friendly to anyone passing through who might have a few bucks to spend on her. I guess she wasn't getting much attention from the old man, but it's all water under the bridge now.''

He was relaying all this in a dispassionate voice, obviously unwilling to be the object of sympathy, but Ann couldn't help saying, ''But who took care of you when she left? You were only a little boy.''

''My older sister did what she could, when she was still home. She would have been twenty-five now. She got into drugs, easy enough to do in my neighborhood, and wound up going to Miami to support her habit. She died of an overdose about ten months ago.''

Although Ann had already gotten most of this from Amy, hearing it come from his mouth as though he were discussing the weather had a chilling effect on her. She sat in silence for so long that he finally said flatly, ''If you're sorry you came up here with me, I'll take you home now.''

Ann ran to fling herself on him, wrapping her arms around his torso and burying her face against his chest. His arms came around her immediately in response, and she heard him sigh, whether in relief or gratitude at her reaction it was impossible to say.

"You know," he said above her head, with a catch in his voice, "you should be more careful. You don't really know me, Princess. I could have brought you up here to rape and murder you."

"Ever since I saw your face when you locked the door of the office at Jensen's garage, I wasn't afraid of you," Ann replied softly. "Only of what I might do because of the way I feel."

His grip tightened and she felt him kiss the top of her head lingeringly.

"Shouldn't I tell you something about me now?" Ann inquired comfortably, closing her eyes.

"I already know about you. Henry Talbot is your father, that's enough."

"Don't you want to know if I have a boyfriend?"

"If you did, you now have a new one," he said confidently, adjusting his position to draw her even closer.

Ann giggled. He might be insecure about his family's varied problems, but regarding his appeal to women he knew that he was on firm ground.

"My friend Amy says that all the girls in Palm High were after you," Ann said.

"Who the hell is Amy?"

"We go to Winfield Academy together. Her cousin, Carol Brady, graduated with you."

"Carol Brady?"

"She was on the cheerleading team. Her father runs the hardware store in Laguna."

"Oh, yeah. Long brown hair, glasses, big mouth."

"That's Carol."

"Well, don't believe everything you hear. People exaggerate. I was never with anybody like you, that's for sure."

Ann sat up and took his hand, lightly tracing the calluses on his palm with her index finger. "But you've had lots of experience, and I haven't had any," she said.

"How old are you, Princess?" he asked quietly, after a thoughtful pause.

"Seventeen. I'll be eighteen in January."

He sighed heavily. "That's what I thought. You're underage in this state."

"You won't stop seeing me!" Ann said in a panic, clutching his hand.

"No, no," he said, pulling her into his arms again. "We just have to go slow and be careful."

"How slow?" she asked, running her lips along the firm line of his throat, feeling powerful and womanly with newfound desire. "How careful?"

He rolled her under him and kissed her wildly, until she was sinking her fingers into his lush hair and wrapping her legs around his hips, urging herself against him. He finally pushed her away and stood abruptly, walking a short distance to lean against a nearby tree, breathing harshly.

"This is going to be tougher than I thought," he said at length, when he was under control again.

"I know I'm not helping," Ann said, not quite ashamed of herself. "I can't keep my hands off you."

"The feeling is mutual." He sat a few feet away from her and said, "I have to ask you a question."

"Anything."

"Did you call Jensen's earlier tonight and ask for me?"

"That was my friend Amy. I wanted to make sure you were there and I was nervous about calling myself."

"Why?"

"I thought you might recognize my voice."

"I would have, I think. But why didn't you just admit that it was you?"

"I wanted the chance to back out if I got cold feet."

"I'm glad you didn't, Princess."

"So am I." She hesitated a moment and then said, "Why do you always call me 'princess'?"

"Because that's what you look like to me, all golden hair and big blue eyes, creamy skin. Like what's her name...with the dwarfs. Snow White."

"Snow White had black hair," Ann said laughing. "At least in the movie, she did."

"Well, then, Sleeping Beauty. Or that other one in the tower, Rapunsa."

"Rapunzel."

"Right. I know she was a blonde—I saw the cartoon." He was laughing with her. He stood, pulled Ann to her feet, and enfolded her tenderly.

"What are we going to do, Rapunzel?" he said into her ear. "I would go over to your house and talk to your father man to man, if I thought it would do any good...."

"Promise me you won't do that, Heath!" Ann cried, seizing his arms. "Promise me!"

"All right, Annie, all right. Take it easy."

"You don't know what he's like. He'll do something awful to you, I know he will. You have to believe me."

"I believe you. I believe you. Relax. Whew! Your old man must be some piece of work."

"I'm supposed to cover his name with glory by marrying some millionaire. He will regard it as a failure on his part if I wind up with anything less."

"Like me, for example."

"I didn't mean it that way. I'm just trying to tell you that talking to him reasonably won't work. I've tried it for years. My older brother has been going crazy trying to live up to the Talbot name since he was born. It's worse for him, being a boy, because he has to inherit the business and prove himself worthy to be chairman of the board."

"And all you have to do is marry well?"

"You got it."

"I didn't know you had a brother."

"He lives in Massachusetts with his mother, my father's first wife. He's in college now, spending the summer as an intern at the Harvard Business School. Usually he's down here this time of year."

"So I guess this discussion means that we have to sneak around, huh?" Heath said bluntly.

"We have no choice. Amy will help, she's very clever. Speaking of Amy, I have to get to her place by midnight, that's her curfew. Her parents will be back home by then and I'm supposed to stay the night at her house."

"Where does she live?"

"Cocoa Boulevard, by the golf course. Her family is moving to Largo in the fall."

"I'll drop you off there," Heath said.

Ann moved back to look at him. "When will I see you again?" she asked him.

"I'm off Tuesday night," he said. "Can you meet me in the parking lot of the Lime Island Inn? So many people come and go there, we won't attract any attention. We'll take a ride out of town and drive someplace where nobody will see us."

"Eight o'clock?" Ann said.

"Seven. That will give us more time together." He kissed her forehead and then said, "Come on, Princess, back in the saddle again. I have to get you back to town."

Riding back to Port Lisbon with her arms planted securely around Heath's middle, Ann knew she was the happiest she had ever been in her life.

During the next six weeks Heath spent every waking minute he wasn't working with Ann. She, in turn, spent sleepless nights thinking up excuses to explain her absences to her parents, called on friends who hadn't heard from her in months to have them cover for her dates with Heath, and even invented a part-time job in Laguna to account for some evenings away from home. She knew she was pushing the limit when her mother began to acquire that "worried" look, common to all parents who suspect their teenage offspring of duping them. But Ann was ecstatic and walking on clouds, and so, deliberately ignored the warning signs.

Reality would not dare interrupt her dream.

She and Heath covered the Keys on his bike, playing pool and pinball and miniature golf, dancing in out-of-the way joints and eating in roadside cafés, generally having a wonderful time. Ann found Heath endlessly interesting; he had led a completely different life from the one she knew and she never tired of listening to his stories. He kept her on the move, because too much time spent alone was dangerous. She was wildly infatuated with him physically, in love for the first time and eager to experiment. He, of course, was more experienced, but also young and in love, and as the broiling summer days passed, his defenses began to weaken and they came closer and closer to the point of no return.

Ann was preparing to leave for her bogus job one evening when her father called her into his study. She knew she was in trouble when she saw her mother hovering anxiously in the hallway and Henry Talbot wearing his no-nonsense, Chief-Executive-Officer-of-ScriptSoft look. Ann walked meekly behind him into the paneled den and sat in the chair he indicated across from his desk.

"What is it, Daddy?" she asked innocently.

"Don't bat your eyelashes at me, young lady. That may work with your hot-blooded, swamp-trotter boyfriend, but it will cut no mustard in this room."

Ann could feel the perspiration begin to trickle down her legs and into her shoes.

"What do you mean?" she said quietly.

"I mean that I know you do not have a job in Laguna. I also know that you have abused my trust, not to mention your mother's trust, by inventing stories to explain your whereabouts while you've been flitting all over these islands with that grease monkey straight from the trash heap—Heath Bodine."

"Heath isn't trash."

"I don't care what he is, young lady, he is not for you. I know his father. I know his family. A worse bunch of layabouts, substance abusers and mendicants never lived. And you have taken up with the very flower of the next generation."

"You can't stop me from seeing him."

"Oh, I beg to disagree. I know where you've been going, who you've been spending time with—"

"You've been *spying* on me?"

"You're my child, Ann, I have to look out for you."

"What did you do, hire a private detective?"

"I already had security men working for my business. It was easy enough to assign them elsewhere."

Ann stared at him until he looked away.

"I love him, Daddy," she said desperately.

"You do not love him—the very idea is preposterous. You come from one of the finest families on this island and he...well, it doesn't merit consideration. I grant you that he is a handsome boy and possesses a certain raffish charm, that's apparent even to me. But I will *not* have you throw away your future on a person without education, breeding or the slightest chance of ever making a decent living."

"That isn't true!" Ann protested. "Heath is talented and has lots of plans—"

"I am not going to discuss this with you any further, Ann!" her father said abruptly, interrupting her. "You are not to see that Bodine boy again. If I find out that you have disobeyed me, I promise you that the consequences for this young man will be dire."

"What would you do?" Ann whispered, her fingers gripping the seat of her chair, her eyes huge.

"You would be wise not to push me to the point of finding out," her father said crisply. "I trust we understand each other. You may go now."

Ann rose like an automaton and walked out of his den, to face her mother waiting in the hall.

Margaret Talbot put her hand on her daughter's shoulder, but Ann shrugged it off miserably. She knew her mother would never disagree with her father about anything, no matter what her private feelings on the matter.

Ann went into her bedroom, slammed the door, and flung herself down on her bed, rigid and dry-eyed, too numb to cry.

What was she going to do?

Chapter 5

"I don't think you understand the situation, Amy," Ann sobbed, wiping her reddened nose with a tissue. "I'm forbidden to see Heath ever again. When I don't show up to meet him at the inn tonight, he's going to wonder what happened to me, and if I know him, he'll go right over to my house. Can you imagine the scene that will take place then?" She fell back on Amy's bed, closing her eyes, which were so swollen from crying they felt tight and sore.

"Take it easy, I have an idea," Amy said, glancing into the hall to make sure Delores, the Horton's maid, was nowhere in earshot. Her parents were out at a party.

"I'll listen to anything," Ann said dully.

"I'll go to the inn's parking lot tonight and tell Heath what happened."

Ann sat up. "Wonderful idea. He'll drive his bike

directly to my father's door and then beat the man senseless.''

''Not if Heath knows he'll be able to see you here,'' Amy replied slyly.

''Amy, what are you talking about?'' Ann asked wearily. ''I told you, my father is having me followed. I can't go anywhere without his knowing about it.''

''He's not having my house watched, is he?'' Amy asked rhetorically.

''I don't know, maybe,'' Ann said wildly. ''He's acting like an operative for the CIA. Amy, I'm desperate. The summer will be over in two weeks and then we have to go back to school. I'll never be able to see Heath.''

''Will you calm down and listen to me?''

''Your parents will tell my father if I meet Heath here,'' Ann said in exasperation, ignoring her. ''They all stick together for this kind of thing, you know that!''

''They won't tell your father if they're not here to see it,'' Amy said triumphantly.

Ann looked at her.

''They're going to Michigan to stay with my Aunt Rita next week. They'll be gone for ten days.''

Ann leaned forward, feeling the first glimmer of hope since the dismal interview with her father. ''But Delores will be here,'' she said, her mind already racing.

Amy shrugged. ''When my parents aren't home, she's off all the time with her boyfriend. Remember when they went to St. Kitts? She showed up for a couple of hours in the morning to clean the house and then was gone the rest of the day. We have sort of a mutual pact of silence—she doesn't ask me what I'm up to and I do the same thing for her.''

Delores was only a few years older than Ann and Amy and was probably sympathetic to their plight.

"When are they leaving?" Ann asked.

"Monday."

"That's a week away!" Ann wailed. "I can't go without seeing Heath for a week!"

"You'll have to. This plan is the best I can do."

Ann thought about it. "Are you sure you can get to Heath tonight?" she asked.

"No problem. I'm supposed to go over to Murchison's, anyway. I'll just stop at the inn on the way."

"And you'll tell him to meet me here when your parents go away?"

"Right."

"How are you going to get him into your house without my father's spies seeing him?"

"I'll talk to him and we'll work something out, don't worry about it. Maybe he can arrive early, hide his bike a few blocks away, then come in through the Cantrell yard. That place looks like a plant nursery—it will give him great cover. As far as you know nobody is following him, right?"

"As far as I know. There must be a limit to what even my father can do."

Amy sat next to Ann on the bed and sighed. "I can't believe the man put a *tail* on you."

"He's crazy. I always knew it. My mother knows it, too, but she's trapped. She's been married to him almost twenty years and she thinks it's too late for her to start over with a new life."

"How did he find out about Heath in the first place?"

"I don't know. I didn't even ask. Probably one of his cronies saw us someplace and ratted. I guess he was bound to find out sooner or later, I was living in a dreamworld to think otherwise."

"You've been living in a dreamworld since you met Heath, Annie," Amy replied. "You're just realizing that now?"

Ann said nothing.

"What time were you supposed to meet Heath tonight?" Amy asked.

"Seven."

"All right. I'll be there."

"And you'll tell him he can meet me here next week?"

"I'll tell him. Let's hope one of my parents doesn't break a leg in the meantime and cancel the trip."

Ann looked stricken.

"Only kidding. My mother won't miss the chance to get together with her sister and dissect the rest of the family. When the plane for Michigan departs, Mom and Pop Horton will be on it."

"I'll pray that they are."

"Now, come with me and wash your face. Things are looking up, kiddo."

Ann followed Amy out of the bedroom.

She hoped that her friend was right.

The week of waiting passed with glacial speed; Ann hung around the house, staring into space with a book propped on her lap or staring at the television with sightless eyes. Margaret Talbot hated to see her daughter so miserable, but any suggestion she made to take Ann's mind off Heath was met with a curt rebuff. Ann was not interested in shopping, tennis, a swim at the club or a picnic on Big Palm Island. She didn't want to buy school clothes, take a drive to Key Largo, pick out tapes at Murchison's or books at Frawley's. In short, she wanted to be left alone, and finally both of her parents did just that, her father satisfied that he had nipped his daughter's declasse relationship in the bud, her mother not so sure about that but maintaining an anxious, concerned silence.

When the day finally arrived for her meeting with Heath, Ann tried not to show her changed mood, moping around as usual and mentioning casually at dinner that she was driving over to Amy's that evening.

"Are you girls going out?" Margaret said brightly, pleased that Ann was demonstrating an interest in leaving the house at last.

"I don't think so. We'll probably just stay in and watch TV, get a pizza. Amy has some new tapes, too."

"That sounds like fun," Margaret chirped, and Ann felt a sharp stab of pity for her mother, who obviously loved her child and wanted her to be happy, but could not reverse two decades of deferring to Henry Talbot. Ann hated lying to her mother but saw no other way to handle her present dilemma.

Ann helped Luisa clear the dinner dishes and then went immediately to her room, where she stared out her window at the swimming pool until it was time to leave.

If she left too early, her father might get suspicious, and the last thing she needed was to have him on the trail again.

Ann breezed past her parents, car keys in hand, at a quarter to seven.

"Have a good time, dear," her mother said, looking up from making a list for round-robin tennis on a yellow legal pad.

Her father lowered his newspaper, glanced at her, then raised it again.

Ann had to exercise extreme self-restraint to drive within the speed limit on her way to Amy's house. When she pulled into the Horton's drive the house looked dark and her heart sank. Had something happened? It looked like nobody was home.

Ann went to the back door and saw Amy standing just inside the screen.

"Is he here?" Ann demanded.

"In my bedroom," Amy replied, opening the door and standing aside.

Ann charged past her and ran down the hall to the bedroom wing, where Heath stood in Amy's doorway. He grinned and Ann flew the last few feet, flinging herself on him.

"Hey," he said, laughing, "slow down." He hugged her tightly and caught Amy's eye over Ann's shoulder. He winked and nodded.

Ann clung to him as if he might vanish.

"Where's your maid?" Heath asked Amy.

"Gone for the night."

He nodded again. There was a long silence and then Amy cleared her throat ostentatiously, saying, "Well, I guess I'll just leave you two kids alone."

"Where are you going?" Ann asked, her voice muffled by Heath's shirt.

"Over to Carol's, she's back from North Carolina."

"Okay to give us till around midnight?" Heath asked.

"Fine. See you then."

Amy slipped out through the patio doors and Heath held Ann off to look at her.

"You've lost weight," he said sternly.

"Just a couple of pounds. What did you expect, Heath? It was hell not being able to see you or even talk to you." She flung her arms around his neck again and he kissed her forehead.

"How did you get in here?" Ann asked him. "Are you sure nobody saw you?"

"Princess, knock off the KGB stuff, will you, please? Your dad is not Big Brother, he can't be watching everybody."

"He was watching *me*. How do you think he found out about us?" Ann countered.

"I know, Amy told me, but I refuse to sneak around like a burglar just because your father has gone nuts."

"Don't underestimate him, Heath, he can hurt us if he wants to—he already has. We haven't seen each other for a week!"

"Yeah, well I'm planning to do something about that," Heath said grimly.

"What do you mean, Heath?" Ann asked, alarm in her tone. "You're not going to do something stupid, are you?"

"Never mind. We're together now, let's enjoy it. Come on over here and sit down with me." He took her by the hand and led her out to the ornate living room, where he sat on the sofa and Ann curled up in his lap.

"Spiffy place," he said, looking around curiously. "Must be nice to have the bucks. Does your house look like this?"

"I guess so. Not quite. My mother's taste is not as . . . well, gaudy."

"What, no gold-fringed lampshades?"

"No." Ann buried her nose under his collarbone and inhaled deeply of his scent. "I missed you so much," she said as his arms came around her again. "Heath, what are we going to do? When will we see each other again?"

"Come on, Princess. We just got here, and you're worrying about that already?"

"Yes, I'm worrying about that already. I can't think about anything else. I'm going back to school soon, ten days or so. What will happen then?"

"I'll come and visit you at school."

"Heath, don't be ridiculous, that place is like Fort Knox. You practically have to take a blood test to show you're a relative to get on the visitors list. I won't be able to see you there."

"Can't you sneak off campus or something?"

"I can try, but if my father warns them, as he surely will, they'll be watching me, supervising my every move. Oh, it's all so complicated I can't stand it."

"We'll work it out."

"How? I don't know what to do, and I'm afraid—" She stopped suddenly.

"What?" Heath said, stroking her hair.

"I'm afraid that you'll get tired of this cloak-and-dagger routine, decide that I'm not worth it. After all, there are plenty of willing girls around, and none of them have Henry Talbot for a father."

"Oh, baby, no. Don't think that. You'll always be worth it, and your father isn't going to keep us apart. I promise you that." He turned her face up for his kiss, and it wasn't long before they were prone on the sofa, the deprivation of the past week escalating into a hunger that neither one of them seemed able to control. Finally Heath tore himself away and sat up, pulling Ann's clinging arms from his neck.

"Baby, we can't do this," he said breathlessly. "It's not right, you're just a kid . . ."

"Oh, and you're Methuselah?"

"I know a lot more about life than you do, and I know you're not ready for this."

"Why?" Ann said, crawling into his lap again. "Am I such a baby? Do I feel like a baby?" She took his hand and placed it on her breast, leaning forward to kiss his neck inside the collar of his shirt.

He groaned and closed his eyes.

"Love me," Ann whispered. "I need you so much. Love me now, please."

He didn't move.

Ann slipped her hand inside the waistband of his jeans and caressed him.

Heath moaned in response and let his head fall back in abandon. Ann worked on him, teasing him into a reaction he knew was reckless but could no longer avoid. In seconds Ann was pinned under him as he became the aggressor, taking the lead in a strong-arm instant that frightened but also thrilled her. He pulled her summer T-shirt over her head and tossed it onto the floor, disposing of her scrap of a bra moments later. He kissed the tanned skin of her bare throat, then moved lower, settling on the pink bud of her nipple. Ann sighed with pleasure and arched her back as he sucked gently, then she gasped as he increased the pressure. She tossed her head from side to side as his lips left her breast and traveled down to her navel, bared by the low waistband of her shorts. His tongue was hot, wet, and her whole being seemed concentrated in the nerve endings he was stimulating. She was flooded with warmth and desire. When he sat up abruptly, she tried to hold him, but he slipped out of her grasp and tore off his shirt, then stepped out of his jeans. She averted her gaze as he undressed, then looked up as he moved to join her.

He was beautiful, his skin a smooth, even shade of light copper, a combination of his heritage and long hours spent in the sun. He was lean but not thin, his arms defined by long, ropy muscles, his abdomen flat, his legs long and trim.

She shuddered with skittish anticipation as he lowered himself to her again. Ann had never known a naked man's full arousal, and she stiffened in shock as he embraced her and ran his hands down the length of her body.

He felt her reaction and said, "Easy, easy," into her ear. Then he kissed her gently, and the surprising softness of his mouth, his muscular arms binding her to him, lulled her back into his spell again. She relaxed as he twined his limbs with hers, turning her toward him and caressing her until she was eager and receptive once more. When she shifted instinctively and felt him ready against her, she pressed into him with an eager innocence that inflamed him. As he unzipped her shorts, she lifted her hips to help him remove her clothes, and then moaned with satisfaction when he slipped his hand between her legs.

"So sweet," he murmured, and she sighed, her face flushed, her brow dewed with perspiration as he stroked her until she wound her legs around his hips, begging for the bliss of total union.

"Are you sure?" he muttered, and Ann looked up at him in a daze of passion, at the ruddy undertone of his amber-hued skin, the sweeping dark lashes shading his eyes. His mouth was moist and swollen from her kisses, parted to show a glimpse of white teeth. She reached up and sank her fingers into his lush hair.

"I love you, Heath. I'm sure."

He pulled her to him tightly, then gasped as she touched him tentatively, encircling him with her fingers. He bit his lip as she trailed the fingers of her free hand over his abdomen, then stroked his thighs, sculpted with muscle. Her touch, light but probing, finally brought him to the limit of his endurance. With one swift movement he positioned her under him, looming above her, his skin hot to the touch and his body taut with tension.

"I want you," he said hoarsely.

"I want you, too," she whimpered, and he took her at her word, entering her in that moment.

Ann froze at the sudden pain, and Heath paused, then pulled back, enfolding her tenderly.

"Are you all right?" he gasped, fighting the overpowering urge to sink into her again.

"I don't know," she said in a small voice.

He rocked her until he felt the tension seep from her body and then began to caress her again, bringing her slowly back to the peak they had approached before. When he entered her the second time she went rigid, then sighed deeply, making a sound of fulfillment that echoed his own.

"Yes?" he said hoarsely, his face buried in the damp curve of her shoulder.

"Oh, yes," she breathed in reply.

He took her at her word.

* * *

"Are you awake?" Heath said softly.

"Mmm," Ann replied luxuriously, stirring and stretching.

"Do you want to take a shower or something? I'm sure Amy wouldn't mind."

"Shower?"

"Are you feeling okay?" Heath asked anxiously.

"Stop fussing, Heath. I'm all right," Ann said, smiling as she got up and looked around on the carpeted floor for her clothes. She handed Heath his crumpled jeans and then slipped quickly into her own shorts and T-shirt.

Silence reigned as they dressed.

"Annie, are you sorry?" Heath finally said desperately, afraid that she regretted what they had done.

She turned and embraced him, kissing his bare shoulder.

"Not for a second," she replied. "I'm just thinking about what we'll do tomorrow. And the day after that."

"I've been thinking, too," Heath said quietly, holding her. "I wasn't going to tell you this just yet, but I didn't realize things would go this far so fast."

Ann drew back to look at him curiously. "What are you talking about?"

"Come here and sit down," Heath said, leading her by the hand back to the sofa they had shared.

Ann sat next to him and waited attentively.

He took a deep breath. "I have a cousin in Georgia who manages a marina there. I've been in touch with him and he says he can give me a job."

All the color drained from Ann's face. "You're moving to Georgia?" she whispered, horrified.

"I'll move if you'll come with me," he replied quietly.

Ann sat perfectly still for a stunned moment, then flung her arms around his neck. "Yes, yes, yes!" she yelled, going weak with relief and joy.

"I've already checked, and seventeen is old enough to get married there. We'll get a place and I'll work full-time. I know it won't be much at first, but we'll be together. That's what's important, right?"

Ann was crying silently, unable to talk, but she nodded vigorously, clutching him.

"The only thing I'd feel bad about is you leaving school...." he said in a worried tone.

"I can take the high school equivalency exam, that's not a problem. I'm sure I could pass it right now," Ann replied, recovering her voice and wiping her eyes with the hem of her T-shirt. "And I can get a job, too, waitressing or something. We'll be just fine, Heath. I know we will."

"Then why are you crying?"

"I'm so happy." She sniffed loudly.

"Look, Princess, I think you should take some time to consider this idea. If you come with me you'd be giving up a lot—your home and security, your whole past life—to go off with a guy with an uncertain future."

She put her hand over his mouth. "My decision is made. Just name the time and the place."

He searched her face and saw that she was serious. He nodded, exhaling forcefully. "Okay. I'll need a couple of days to work out the details. Once we get to Georgia, we can stay with my cousin until we find an apartment. It will probably be crowded at first—he has a couple of kids, but he said that there's a spare bedroom fixed up in the basement.''

"Oh, Heath, I don't care, I don't care," Ann said, kissing him wildly. "I've been going crazy, wondering how we would work this out, wondering how I would ever be able to see you, and here's our solution!" She laughed delightedly.

"I have enough money saved for bus fare for both of us, and if I sell my bike I'll have more..."

"Don't sell your bike!" Ann said, aware of how much he loved it. "Can't we ride it there?"

"It won't exactly be the most comfortable trip," Heath said dryly.

"That's all right."

"You can only bring one duffel bag to put on the back of the bike," he said warningly.

"That's fine. Anything you say."

"I can let you know through Amy when and where to meet me," he said, his arms tightening around her.

"Good."

"We'll do it," he said, his tone confident.

"We will," she echoed, her lips curving unconsciously into a smile again.

All her problems were solved.

Three days later Ann was packing her single bag by the glow of a flashlight when her bedroom door opened and her father snapped on the overhead light.

Her throat closed at the sight of him.

"What do you think you're doing?" Henry Talbot said to his daughter.

Ann decided to confront him. He would have to know sooner or later, it might as well be now.

"Packing," she said calmly.

"To go where?"

"To Georgia with Heath. I'm of age to get married there and he has a job at his cousin's marina. I suppose you know something about this or you would be asleep, not standing here in the middle of the night demanding an explanation."

"Luisa overheard one of your phone conversations with Amy, and she alerted me."

"Is she on your spy payroll now, too?"

"She's very fond of you, Ann, and doesn't want to see you get into trouble. She did the right thing."

"I'm not getting into trouble, I'm getting married."

"No, you're not."

"Yes, I am. Seventeen is old enough to get a license in Georgia. You can't stop me."

"I certainly can. Seventeen is still minority in Florida, and I believe your paramour is of majority age. That means any intercourse between the two of you constitutes statutory rape. If he takes you across state lines, as you say he plans to, he is also in violation of the Mann Act. If you leave this house tonight to meet him, I will have him arrested within an hour."

Ann felt her flesh go cold at his dispassionate tone. She had heard it before in reference to his business dealings, and she knew he meant every word.

"You can't prove anything," she finally answered, keeping her voice steady, trying not to show how frightened she was. "I'll never give evidence against Heath."

"If necessary, I will bring in a doctor to confirm that what I suspect is true," her father said flatly. "But I doubt that you will let things go that far. If you care about this boy at all, you won't want to see him in jail. And I assure you that if you pursue this foolishness, that is exactly where he will land. The usual sentence for statutory rape is several years, I understand."

Ann sat heavily on the edge of her bed, her packing forgotten. "What do you want?" she said dully.

"I have already arranged for you to stay with Mildred Plunkett. You remember my friend in Massachusetts. I called her earlier this evening. I want you to leave for New England in the morning—I'll take you to the airport myself. I will arrange a transfer to the Hampton School for Girls in Longmeadow for the September term. You will leave without ever seeing this boy again, and you will not communicate with him in the future. Please remember that I can raise the rape charge at any point. Don't consider contravening me, or Heath Bodine will pay dearly for your defiance."

Ann stared past him hopelessly, feeling all her plans and hopes shattering like delicate crystal, the shards collecting at her feet. She pictured Heath waiting for her at the appointed spot, waiting for hours in vain, finally realizing that she wasn't coming, thinking that she had abandoned him. It was too awful; she couldn't let it happen. But then she pictured him in handcuffs, languishing in jail, then on trial for a serious crime. That was worse.

There was no way out but to obey.

She looked at her father as a sentenced convict might look at his executioner.

"I'll do whatever you say," she said.

Ann came home from school at Christmas break to find that Heath was gone. She heard from the Jensens that he had joined the navy. He had left them no forwarding address.

Ann had never known the name of Heath's cousin in Georgia. Heath's father would not talk to her. Henry Talbot discussed everything but his daughter's slight lapse in romantic judgment. Margaret Talbot looked on with worried eyes and said very little. Luisa pretended that she knew nothing about the whole episode.

Ann never contacted Heath because she was afraid of what her father would do to him. And she never saw Heath again.

Chapter 6

Ann sat up suddenly as a loud knock at her door pierced her reverie and brought her back to the present. She glanced at the clock on the inn's bedside table.

She had been sitting in the armchair, lost in the past, for more than two hours.

She shook out her left leg as she walked to the door; it was stinging with pins and needles, numb from remaining in the same position for so long. She pulled the door open and saw a room service attendant standing in the corridor next to a rolling cart set lavishly with an elaborate dinner.

"For Miss Talbot," the waiter said, glancing at the number on the door when her expression revealed her surprise.

"I didn't order this," Ann said.

He picked up the slip stuck under an ivory china bud vase containing a single rose. "It's complimentary, from a Miss Amy Horton. The order was placed at one-thirty this afternoon.''

Ann smiled. Amy was determined to get her to eat, one way or another.

''All right, you can bring it in,'' Ann said, tightening the belt on her robe and pushing back her hair. She stepped aside as he wheeled the cart into her room and then she fished in her purse for a tip. When he had left her alone, she lifted the shiny silver covers from the dishes and discovered that Amy had ordered enough food for an army—soup and salad, main dish and vegetables, dessert and coffee, not to mention rolls and butter and various garnishes. It was a feast.

Ann sighed. Dear Amy. She just couldn't seem to understand that availability of food was not the problem; it was complete lack of appetite.

But after this gesture, Ann felt she had to try.

She dutifully sat down in front of the cart and picked up a roll, beginning to eat.

Heath Bodine put down the computer printout he was trying to read and sat back in his chair. He looked around the office of Bimini's Big Palm marina, aware that he would not get any work done today. This pit stop had been a waste of time.

The phone at his elbow rang and the secretary in the outer office picked it up. He watched the red light blink and then switch off without interest.

Since he'd left Harold Caldwell's office he'd been unable to think of anything but his meeting with Ann and the proposal he had made to her. And then when he'd checked in with his Miami branch and heard that she'd left him a message there, he'd known that he had won.

She was going to do what he wanted.

It was curious how little satisfaction that piece of knowledge gave him.

After waiting eleven years to take revenge for Ann's betrayal, he'd thought that the success of his well-planned scheme would taste a little sweeter.

Perhaps the lack of savor resulted from Ann's defeated air, the obvious fragility of the woman who'd confronted him in the lawyer's office. She had always seemed delicate—it was part of what had first attracted him to her—but now she looked...haunted, ethereal, unhappy. He supposed that it was only to be expected, with her family's company on the ropes and her brother in jail. But he had still anticipated some vestige of the old, feisty Ann, always ready to take on her father, the town, the entire universe, anyone who might separate her from her down-scale lover across the tracks.

But of course, that image wasn't the real Ann, or she would never have left him pacing the Big Palm bus station for twelve hours, watching the sunrise and the day begin, looking for her every time the door opened. He remembered the commuters with their paper cups of steaming coffee, the mothers dragging unwilling toddlers toward family visits, the single travelers passing him with closed faces. He'd been unable to acknowledge that she wasn't coming until he'd finally fallen asleep and woken to the gathering dusk to find himself still alone.

Then he'd sped back to Lime Island on his bike, the tears streaming down his face, to find Ann's house closed and dark, a padlock on the garage. He'd torn

out of the driveway and gone straight to Luisa Sanchez's house in Hispaniola. Her face expressionless,
she'd told him that Ann had transferred to a new
boarding school in Massachusetts and her parents had
gone to their vacation home in Maine for several
weeks. She didn't know anything more.

Amy Horton was no help; whatever had caused
Ann to change her plans, she hadn't told Amy about
it before she'd left.

End of story.

He had joined the navy the next day.

Heath rubbed the bridge of his nose, thinking
about that break with Ann, the way it had formed the
rest of his life. With his background, it had been difficult for him to trust anyone, but she had somehow
slipped inside the barriers his nineteen-year-old self
had erected against the world and won his heart.

Then, when Daddy Talbot crooked his imperious
finger, she had tossed that heart away as if it were
garbage.

What had happened? Had she thought about what
it would be like to live without the cushion of the
Talbot money and developed cold feet? Probably.
Romantic daydreams were one thing, but reality was
quite another.

And then, of course, there was the payoff. He
couldn't let himself forget about that.

Knuckles rapped on the door of the office. Joe
Jensen pulled the door open and stuck his head inside the gap he'd created.

"Heath, we have to talk about the Sea Ray inventory. I've got several used twenty-footers that need a
markdown, will you come and take a look?" Jensen
said.

"Be right there," Heath replied. He stood abruptly, thinking ahead to his dinner the next night with Ann.

He *would* marry her, and make her pay for everything.

Ann changed three times for her meeting with Heath, not even sure why she was doing it. Some vestige of their earlier relationship made her want to look nice for him, even though she knew that the subject on his mind would hardly be romance. Everything she owned was now too big for her, but she settled on a blue silk shirtwaist that fit reasonably well, wearing it with high-heeled pumps and her mother's pearls. She brushed out her hair, checked her lipstick for the last time, and finally left her room, her hands blocks of ice from nervousness as she descended in the elevator.

Heath was already seated in the inn's dining room, a glass of Scotch on the table in front of him. He rose as she approached him and held out a chair for her, his face unsmiling. She sat and looked at him across the table, which was covered with a white linen cloth and illuminated by a candle set in a small hurricane lamp.

"Have you been waiting for me a long time?" she asked.

"For eleven years," he said.

She looked at him.

"Just a few minutes," he amended. "Would you like something to drink?"

Ann shook her head. He was wearing a raw silk blazer, obviously expensive, that fit him like a glove, with an ivory shirt, striped tie and brown slacks. He looked every inch the successful businessman, a far cry from the impoverished teenager she had known. But she saw that boy in the features that had not changed—the high cheekbones, the seal-black hair, the almond-shaped amber eyes. Oh, Heath, she thought, feeling the fullness of tears in her throat. She blinked and looked away.

Heath folded his hands on the table and said, "I think you should know there have been a few developments in your brother's case. I assumed that you wanted to see me in order to agree to my plan, so I took some preliminary steps. First thing this morning I contacted Trevor Hankins in New York, and he called the judge who refused to free Tim on bail. Hankins has arranged for a new bail hearing on Thursday and will be flying in to represent Tim at the proceeding. Hankins feels confident that he can spring Tim within twenty-four hours, and I will put up a cash bond for whatever amount the judge demands."

It took several seconds for Ann to absorb the information. "You're very efficient," she finally said quietly.

"Money talks," he replied shortly. "I've also contacted the board of directors at ScriptSoft to see if I can make a loan to the company in exchange for their dropping of the mismanagement suit against your brother. I'll buy up the existing stock if I have to, bring in a reorganization team, whatever is necessary. I'm confident something can be arranged."

Ann watched him, waiting.

"That won't get rid of the feds, of course, the SEC is a law unto itself. But Hankins has a colleague who specializes in white-collar crime and I can assure you that Tim will have the best defense money can buy if the stock tampering case comes to trial.''

Ann swallowed. "Thank you.''

He took a sip of his drink, rattling the ice in the glass. "I keep *my* promises,'' he said.

The emphasis on the third word was not lost on her. "And in exchange for all of this you want . . . ?'' Ann said.

"You. Just you.''

"Can't you let it go, Heath?'' Ann asked softly. "I'll find some way to pay you back for all of this, but a marriage that will make us both miserable seems—'' She broke off, at a loss.

"Too high a price to pay?'' he suggested.

A waiter arrived with a platter of appetizers and set it down between them, oblivious to the mood of the diners.

"I took the liberty of ordering something for us,'' Heath said, taking another small swallow of his drink.

"Will there be anything else at the moment, sir?'' the waiter inquired.

"No, thank you. We'll order later.''

The waiter left, and Heath looked around expansively. "Lots of memories in this place, huh, Princess? Well, out in the parking lot, at any rate.''

"Heath, don't.''

"Why not? Are we going to pretend that none of it happened? That's a pretty tall order, don't you think?''

"I never meant to hurt you.''

"I see. You thought that leaving me walking in circles in the Big Palm bus station waiting for somebody who never came was going to make me happy?''

"You don't know what happened that night, you never have!" Ann protested.

He sat back and surveyed her cynically. "Why don't you tell me? I know you're just dying to tell me your sanctified version, it should be very interesting."

Ann ignored his tone and said, "My father interrupted me in the middle of the night as I was packing to go and meet you. Luisa had overheard a conversation I'd had with Amy and alerted him that I was leaving. He told me that if I tried to leave town with you he would have you arrested for statutory rape."

Heath's face was unreadable. "And?" he inquired, raising an eyebrow.

"Isn't that enough? If I didn't promise to transfer to that school in New England and never see you again, you would have wound up in jail!" Ann said heatedly.

"Ah, I see. Very noble of you. Self-sacrifice and all of that. Just like Romeo and Juliet. Or was it Laurel and Hardy?"

Ann stared at him in consternation. It was clear he didn't believe her.

"How can you sit there, all prim and proper with your bare face hanging out, and lie to me like this, Princess?" he said, his tone deadly. Dangerous.

"I'm not lying!" she said, amazed that he could doubt her. "That's exactly what happened!"

He picked up his glass again and drained it. "I guess I never told you about my father's sister Elsie, did I?" he said neutrally.

Ann gazed at him, bewildered. What on earth was he talking about now?

"My father was the black sheep of his family. The rest of his siblings actually work, go food shopping, take showers, remain vertical after 4:00 p.m. You know, they do the normal things. My Aunt Elsie, for example, worked as the secretary to a trust officer in a Miami bank. As luck would have it, the very bank where your daddy did the bulk of his business."

Ann waited, sure that there was a point to this ramble and sooner or later Heath would get to it.

"Now I was fond of Elsie—she was the one relative who lived near enough to visit and take the occasional interest in me. She happened to arrive the day after your abrupt departure on one of her periodic checks to see if my father was still alive, and I'm afraid in my distress I blurted out the whole ugly tale of our somewhat star-crossed relationship. So Elsie was very interested when, one week after you decamped, she found herself typing up forms for her boss that released to you the sum of one hundred thousand dollars. The person countersigning the form was none other than your father."

Ann looked back at him, baffled, trying to follow him. What the devil was this?

"Quite a payoff for dumping the boyfriend, wasn't it, Princess? I knew you were desperate to get away from your father, and taking off with me was one way of doing it, but in the end it must have been impossible to give up all the fine things that the Talbot money could buy.... Why settle for a Georgia hut with a teenage mechanic husband when a plush boarding school in stately New England awaits you, with the cushion of a hundred grand to make dumping the grease monkey worth your while? You found a way to get away from your old man and actually

have him finance your exit! I applaud your ingenu-
ity, Ann. I never would have guessed you had it in
you."

Ann was speechless, trying to put together the
pieces of the puzzle. Suddenly, she remembered.

"You're talking about the trust fund," she said.

He studied her, his expression glacial.

"My grandmother had set up a trust find to finance my education and made my father the trustee.
The tuition at the Hampton school was much higher
than at my previous school and so my father peti-
tioned the trustee to release the money to me, on
condition that I use it for my boarding school tuition
and put aside the remainder for college, which I did."

He said nothing.

"Don't you see? He wanted to pack me off but he
didn't want to pay for it himself. Invading the trust
fund was his neat, financially sound solution. The
timing of it was just a coincidence. I didn't know his
plan for footing the bill. My father didn't pay me off
to leave you, Heath, he was just using my grandmother's money to stash me away in Massachusetts!
If I had tried to use a penny of it to get back to you he
would have been on the phone to the police in a second. I'm sorry if you thought the money was a bribe,
but that simply isn't true."

He stared back at her stonily. She might as well
have been talking to herself.

"You still don't believe me, do you?" she said
sadly. "You haven't really changed at all. Eleven
years ago you could never quite accept that I would
throw in my lot with you, and when I didn't show up
the night we had planned to run away, you were only

too willing to jump to conclusions and think the worst of me."

"So it's all *my* fault now?" he said. "You're a blameless angel and I'm the bastard who had no faith in you?" He laughed bitterly and looked away, shaking his head, as if she were just too ridiculous to credit.

"I loved you, Heath. I have never loved anyone like that again. The only thing that could have separated me from you was fear for your safety. If you choose to think otherwise, there isn't much I can do about it, is there?"

He signaled for the waiter to bring him another drink. "It's interesting how you've made yourself the heroine of our grim little drama," he said. "It's even more interesting that nobody is left alive to contradict you. Hardly more than a decade has passed and, except for us, all the major players have died—your father, your mother, even poor, deluded Luisa."

"Amy is alive."

"Amy will say anything you tell her to say."

Ann gave a brief, mirthless laugh. "You don't know Amy very well."

"Apparently I didn't know you very well, either. I fell like a ten-ton weight for your poor-little-rich-girl act and you used me for your own purposes until you got exactly what you wanted."

"And what was that, in your estimation?" Ann asked quietly, her eyes never leaving his face.

"Escape!" he said. "Escape from Casa Talbot, where your crazy old man ruled you and your mother like Draco."

"Escape to a boarding school in New England that was more like a jail than an institution of higher learning! I would rather have been in a tar-paper shack with you, Heath, and that's the truth."

"Yeah, I'm sure it was hell," he said sarcastically. "I've seen pictures of that place they sent you. I remember the layout—lots of grass, lots of trees, a green campus dotted with white-columned mansions separated by brick pathways. It sure looked like marine boot camp to me."

"Appearances can be deceiving," Ann said.

The waiter appeared with a fresh drink for Heath and said, "Ready to order now?"

"I'll call you when we're ready to order," Heath snarled, not looking at him.

The waiter looked startled, glanced sidelong at Ann, then beat a hasty exit.

"Look," Heath said, "I'm not going to sit here and listen to you defend what you did, especially when you characterize it as a selfless gesture to keep me out of jail. Actually, I can't believe you have the nerve to try to pass this bogus story off as the truth. You must think I'm still as stupid as I was back when I thought that old Harley and you were all I needed to be happy. This highly inventive tale must be an example of your writer's imagination."

"You know I'm a writer?" Ann said.

"I have your first book."

"Why?"

"Oh, I've always kept track of you, which is obviously more than you can say about me."

"It was too painful to hear anything about you, Heath. The only way I could survive was by burying all of it."

"Here's to the buried past," he said, saluting her with his liquor glass.

Ann pushed her chair back from the table. "Heath, this is pointless. You don't want to hear anything I have to say." She picked up her purse.

"If you leave, I will get on the phone and cancel everything I did for your brother this morning," he said calmly. "All it takes is a word from me and he stays right where he is."

Ann resettled in the chair. "It must be wonderful to have such power," she said.

"I earned it," he replied. "Since you seem anxious to leave, I think I should lay out the terms of our agreement."

"Oh, by all means."

"We will be getting married on Friday afternoon of this week," he began.

"Friday?" she gasped. "So soon?"

"Do you need time to buy a trousseau?" he asked dryly.

She said nothing.

"I have already arranged an appointment with the clerk's office for the ceremony. We can do the blood tests tomorrow. Joe Jensen and his wife can serve as the witnesses at the wedding."

"Joe Jensen of Jensen's Marina?"

"He works for me now."

"So you didn't forget all of your old friends."

"Only the ones who forgot me," he shot back.

Ann sighed and bit her lip. How much more of this could she take? More importantly, could she take it every day? But the alternative was too horrible to contemplate. She was trapped.

"You will keep up appearances," Heath went on. "Serve as my hostess for the annual Christmas party for my employees, accompany me to the social functions I must attend in consideration of my postion as CEO of Bimini. No one is to know how things really stand, or I will consider it a breach of our pact.''

Ann listened dolefully, not looking at him.

"And in case you're loath to raise this delicate subject, I want to make something clear. Ours will *not* be a marriage in name only. You will sleep with me anytime I want, in any place I want, just like a dutiful little wife."

"That *is* a marriage in name only, Heath. Without a relationship to back it up, sex alone doesn't make a marriage."

"Giving advice to the lovelorn now? Why don't you write a column for the papers, like Dear Abby? You apparently have the talent for it."

"What else?" she asked tersely, igoring the gibe.

"You will live with me in my house, and not take off every five minutes for visits to relatives or whatever else you can think of to get away from me. I expect you to be around and available, do you understand?"

"Where do you live?"

He drank deeply. "I bought the Curtis house on Prospect Boulevard," he said.

Ann was silent. Duncan Curtis had been a friend of her father's, the owner of a stucco, Spanish-style waterfront mansion that was arguably the only home on Lime Island more impressive than Henry Talbot's.

"I didn't know that Duncan Curtis had moved away," she finally said.

"He retired to Southern California two years ago, to be near his daughter," Heath replied shortly.

"And you rushed right in and bought his house."

"Why not?"

"I see now why you want to marry me, why torturing me outside the bonds of holy matrimony would not be sufficient for you," Ann said quietly.

"What are you talking about?" he replied, swallowing the rest of his drink in one gulp.

"It's all part of the master plan, isn't it? The plan to show the Lime Island old-timers—whoever's left, anyway—that the poor boy from the wrong side of the tracks has made good, big time. The best house on the island, the billboards for Bimini plastered on every available surface, the good works documented in the newspapers, and now marriage to the daughter of the most prominent man, the one they all remember from the country club in the old days. It has little to do with me—I'm just a means to an end."

"It has *everything* to do with you," he said quietly. "Make no mistake about that."

"They really hurt you, didn't they, Heath? Those golf-playing snobs in their pastel polo shirts. More than even I suspected."

"They never hurt me as much as you did. They couldn't. You were the only one I ever loved, the only one I ever let get close enough to see that I had those feelings. And you made sure that you threw it all back in my face."

She put her hand over his on the table.

He withdrew his hand immediately.

"Do you understand what I want?" he inquired tonelessly, his features immobile.

"Perfectly," she replied.

"Good. Will you be staying here at the inn until the day of the wedding?"

"Yes. Since my brother's disgrace, all doors seem closed to me. I imagine you know the feeling."

"Very well. I'll call you to arrange a time to go for the blood tests."

"Am I dismissed?" she asked crisply.

"Not quite yet. We have to discuss the honeymoon."

"The honeymoon?" Ann said faintly.

"Of course. Don't you want go somewhere secluded and romantic to enjoy your new husband?"

"No."

"Too bad. Because I plan to get my money's worth, starting with a week in Caneel Bay. We'll fly out right after the wedding."

"You're enjoying this immensely, aren't you, Heath?" Ann said quietly.

"This?"

"Torturing me."

"Not many people would consider a week at a Caneel Bay resort to be torture," he said mildly.

"And am I supposed to play the role of the ecstatic honeymooner?" Ann demanded.

"That shouldn't be too much trouble for you. As I recall, you're very good at role-playing. You convinced me that you were madly in love with me without too much difficulty."

She looked away from him. "Is there anything else?" she said tensely.

He nodded. "The Curtis house, which is now the Bodine house, is at 1223 Prospect. If I were you, I would arrange to have anything you want from your apartment shipped there. Do you have anyone in New York who can pack for you?"

"I left a key with a neighbor. I can ask her to put together a few things for me."

"Good. Better ask her to send them express—we're booked on a flight out to the islands Friday night."

"Should I sublet my apartment?"

He shrugged. "It doesn't matter. I'll buy out your lease if you like."

Ann smiled thinly. Having money obviated quite a number of considerations.

He must have known what she was thinking because he said, "Turnabout is fair play, no?"

"I don't think you know much about fair play anymore, Heath," Ann replied.

He stared at her for a long moment, then said neutrally, "You may go now."

Ann rose on shaky legs and walked out of the dining room.

Chapter 7

Ann's wedding day dawned beautiful and clear, as if nature were playing a joke at her expense. She had purchased a lovely suit for the occasion, off-white with a fitted jacket embroidered at the cuffs and along the shawl collar with tiny seed pearls, worn with a silk camisole and a short, slim skirt. She donned the outfit on Friday with grim determination, vowing that she would not show up for the ceremony bedraggled and weeping; she would not give Heath the satisfaction. She piled her hair on top of her head, added her mother's pearls to her ears and neck, and picked up her purse.

Heath might hate her, but he would never be able to say she was a coward.

She had just walked down the front steps of the inn when his sleek Italian sports car glided to a stop at the curb. He got out and held the door for her, saying, "No luggage?"

"I only brought one bag from New York. I didn't think I would be staying on Lime Island very long."

"I'll send somebody for it," he said shortly. He was wearing a conservative suit that made him look more dashing than ever; the contrast with his businesslike clothes and his dark, almost piratical coloring was devastating.

Ann slipped into the bucket seat of the car and stared straight ahead, thinking that he seemed to have an army of minions with nothing to do but his bidding.

The ride to the registry office was short. They walked up the steps to the concrete building side-by-side in silence. Ann had expected nothing different; they had completed the blood tests and license application while barely exchanging a word.

Inside, the Jensens were sitting together on a bench. Joan held a large orchid corsage in a florist's plastic box on her lap. They both rose when they saw Heath and Ann come through the door.

"Well, there she is!" Joe Jensen caroled, and enfolded Ann in a backbreaking bear hug. "Prettiest little girl I ever saw. I always tell Heath that."

When he released Ann, Joan kissed her on the cheek and handed her the corsage. "We're so happy to be part of your special day," she said, beaming.

Ann looked at Heath, who turned away.

He had obviously not told the Jensens the details surrounding this happy event.

Ann stood patiently while the older woman pinned the corsage to the shoulder of her wedding suit and then patted the flower with satisfaction.

"There now. That's just the touch you needed," Joan said. "I knew Heath wouldn't think of it."

Mercifully, the door to the registry office opened and the clerk called their names.

The spare, paneled walls of the judge's chamber did little to lift Ann's spirits once they were inside. Someone had decided to get a jump on Christmas and had hung a huge green wreath decorated with holly berries and a fat, glittering silver bow over the registry desk. Ann stared at it as the justice put on his glasses and examined their documents, then began to read. As he droned on, Ann tuned out, and so she was surprised when Heath suddenly took her hand and slipped onto her finger a slim, etched gold band. She hardly had time to recover from the thought that he had selected it for her when she found herself accepting a thicker band from him and putting it on his finger. Her eyes met Heath's and he held her gaze for a second, then looked back at the person marrying them. Ann felt her throat tighten as she heard the justice talk a little more and then say, "You may now kiss the bride."

Heath turned to her and kissed her.

Ann hadn't felt the touch of his lips in eleven years, but the memory was so strong it seemed like eleven minutes. Despite the circumstances, she felt herself yearning toward him, and when he pulled back, she felt such a sense of loss that she had to turn away to mask her expression. She blinked rapidly, sniffing, until the tears had vanished from her eyes.

Afterward, Ann remembered little of the ceremony's conclusion. It had been such a far cry from the wedding she had dreamed of as a girl that she blocked it out, accepting the congratulations and warm wishes of the Jensens with a wooden smile. Heath must have said something appropriate to them because they melted away with cheerful waves and she found herself back in the car with him in a matter of minutes.

"What did you tell them?" Ann asked as he shifted gears and gunned the motor.

"I told them we had been apart so long that we wanted to get right on with the honeymoon."

"Didn't they think that was rather a sparse wedding for a multimillionaire?" she inquired.

"They know I value my privacy," he replied shortly.

Ann let her head fall back against the leather headrest, wondering where they were going. Her life seemed to be out of her hands since she'd met Heath again.

Her question was answered as he turned down Prospect Boulevard and then pulled into the long, curving driveway of the house once belonging to Duncan Curtis. The landscaping was different, more elaborate than Ann's memory of it. Curtis had never made the estate a showplace to be envied, but it was clear that Heath wanted Lime Island residents to know that its new owner was a man who had definitely "arrived."

Heath used a remote control to open one of the triple garage doors and pulled the sleek car into the middle bay. The garage was antiseptically clean, a tier of shelves against one plaster wall containing antifreeze and motor oil the only color in the whitewashed environment. The bay to the right contained an RV; the one to the left, an elaborate Harley Heath could never have afforded in his Jensens' Marina days. Ann was sure there were several boats anchored out back in the lagoon and maybe even a plane stashed somewhere.

"He who dies with the most toys wins," Ann said softly, glancing around her.

Heath shot her a look as he turned off the motor. "What is that supposed to mean?" he said.

"Has all this shiny machinery made you happy, Heath?" Ann inquired.

"It hasn't made me unhappy, which is more than I can say for you," he replied.

"Still a Harley man, I see," she said, deciding to ignore the riposte.

"Always," he replied, and got out of the car, coming around to open the door for her before leading her into the house.

The garage entered into the kitchen, and Ann paused on the threshold, struck by the transformation the house had undergone since she had last seen it.

Heath had gutted the place, eliminated walls and raised the roof, introducing a Native American motif that carried through the newly enlarged, now airy rooms. She walked across the tiled floor, passing the gleaming appliances and double refrigerator, through the dining area, with its varicolored Seminole rug on the wall and carved oak chairs, into the living room, where the modern furniture centered around another rug of Native American design spread on the pegged pine floor. She looked around in reverential silence for a few moments and then said, "This is gorgeous, Heath."

He said nothing. The sincerity of her remark was obvious.

"But where are the people?" Ann added.

He looked at her.

"You've created an appropriate setting, but you're alone here. This house looks like a museum."

"I'm never here," he said stiffly. "In the past I've stayed mostly at my town house in Miami."

"Then why buy this place here? To prove to the townies that you could?" Ann asked.

"I do as I damn well please—I don't have to justify myself to you," he replied, not looking at her.

"Who takes care of this place?"

"I employ a couple who live in the guest house out back. I gave them the week off when I knew we were getting married."

"Didn't want any witnesses to the torture?" Ann said. "Afraid Amnesty International would come after you?"

He walked over to the liquor trolley by the bay window and poured himself two fingers of Scotch.

"You've changed, Princess. You never used to indulge in self-pity," he said.

The telephone rang.

"Does anybody know we're here?" Ann asked.

"I left word at my office that we would be stopping off at the house. You might want to check in the den to the left of the front hall—I had your boxes put in there when they arrived from New York. See if everything you need is there."

Heath went to the kitchen to answer the phone and Ann walked out of the living room and into the hall, which was floored with terra-cotta terrazzo tiles and filled with tall, standing plants. Sunlight flooded in through the floor-to-ceiling windows and reflected off the Seminole shields on the walls. She got the same feeling here as in the rest of the house; it was beautiful and perfectly assembled, but cold. Had Heath changed so much that an environment like this one was now acceptable, even desirable?

She moved into the den and slit the tape on the boxes with a brass letter opener she found on the desk. It didn't take her long to determine that her neighbor had sent the clothes and personal effects she had requested, including her computer disks, but the specially packed computer box had not arrived.

"Everything there?" Heath said from the doorway.

"Everything except my computer. I need it to work."

"Do you have the disks?"

"Yes."

"Then buy another computer." He took out his wallet and extracted a credit card from it, tossing the card onto the desk. "There's a computer store on Big Palm. We'll be going there, anyway, so you can stop off and get whatever you need."

"Why will we be going to Big Palm?" Ann asked.

"The honeymoon's over, Princess. Something's come up. I have to be at a meeting tomorrow, so the trip to Caneel Bay is off."

Ann didn't even try to disguise the relief she felt.

"You don't seem devastated by this piece of information," he said dryly.

"I'm not."

"Why?"

"I wasn't exactly up for Honeymoon Heaven. To have to be with other people obviously in love, when we're..."

"In hate?" he suggested. "I've booked the bridal suite at the Imperial Plaza for tonight," he said, smiling at her change of expression. "We'll stay there until Daniela and Victor return."

"Why can't we stay here?" Ann said wearily.

"There's no food in the house, nobody to cook it if there were," he replied.

"I'm not helpless, Heath. I can go to a store and operate a stove, and for that matter—"

"No," he said quietly.

Ann subsided. If he was determined to play out this charade, there was little she could do but go along with it.

"Do you want to pack some of your things?" he asked. "There's a suitcase in the bedroom."

Ann followed him down the hall to what was obviously his room. By stark contrast with the rest of the house, it was an almost Spartan chamber lined with bookshelves and featuring a king-size bed covered with a plain, striped quilt.

"There's a dressing room through there," he said, pointing. "You can use the closet and chest of drawers. This bed, of course, you will be sharing with me."

Ann felt her scalp tingle at his dispassionate description of their connubial bliss. She went into the dressing room and found the valise sitting on a chair.

He had, apparently, thought of everything.

When she returned he had discarded his tie and was carrying an overnight bag in his hand.

"Ready?" he said.

Ann nodded. She didn't feel ready, but then, for what he had in mind, she never would.

As he backed the car out of the garage Heath said to her, "Didn't it strike you as odd that I didn't have you sign a prenuptial agreement? I'm worth quite a bit of money, you know."

"Yes, Heath, I know. You've made that very clear."

"Well?"

"I'm sure you have it covered," Ann said wearily.

"That's right, I do. So don't get any ideas about ditching me after a few months and walking away with a fortune, you'll find that my lawyers can make that very difficult. You can understand my concern, since ditching me was one of your areas of expertise, as I recall."

Ann ignored him, staring out the window as they drove across the causeway. She tried to imagine that she was with Heath under pleasant circumstances, anticipating an evening that would end with them going home together like a normal couple. The contrast with reality was too painful and she gave up the fantasy, turning to look at him as he drove with the single-minded attention she remembered him giving to mending boat engines when they were younger.

His profile was grim, but clean as a coin's, his mouth firm, his nose arched and strong, his lush hair spilling onto his forehead. Just the sight of him made her heart beat faster. Why couldn't he be less desirable? she wondered. Why couldn't he have gotten fat or bald or somehow less attractive, so she could just close her eyes and think of England, like those Victorian ladies with portly husbands who did their British duty? But she still wanted Heath too much, still thrilled whenever he touched her, and it was going to be hard work not to fall desperately in love with him all over again, no matter how badly he treated her. She couldn't help thinking that the real Heath was still in there somewhere—the passionate, headstrong Heath she had known, hiding behind the facade of this sarcastic, bloodless millionaire.

He turned and caught her staring at him.

"What are you thinking?" he asked sharply.

"Just that you haven't changed very much."

"You're wrong there. I have."

"I meant physically."

"Neither have you. A little skinnier, maybe."

Ann let that pass.

"Do you enjoy what you do?" he asked suddenly.

"What?"

"The writing. Do you enjoy it?"

"Yes. Very much."

"Why?"

"Well, the research takes me away. It's almost like living in the time and place I'm studying when I'm preparing the work. And then writing the story is like . . ." she hesitated.

"Dreaming on paper?" he suggested.

Ann smiled. "Yes, exactly. Dreaming on paper."

"That should suit you just fine. You always had your head in the clouds," he said. "Your brother couldn't have shipped ScriptSoft out from under you if you had been paying the slightest bit of attention to what he was doing."

"I never cared what he did with the company, Heath."

"Why not? It was your money he was throwing away, too, wasn't it?"

"I didn't want to be reminded of my life in Florida, of my father, of any of it."

"Or of me."

"I never forgot you," Ann said softly. "How could I?"

"I don't know, Annie, my phone wasn't ringing. Seems like you forgot me easily enough."

"I went to see your father when I came home from school that Christmas," Ann said, wondering why she was still trying to convince him when his mind was obviously closed on this subject. "He wouldn't talk to me."

"Couldn't is more like it. I assume that he was dead drunk at the time?"

"He seemed—" She stopped.

"Sloshed?" Heath supplied.

"I guess so."

"And abusive."

"Yes."

Heath sighed. "Yes, that was dear old dad. He finally died of cirrhosis while I was in the navy. I sent Elsie a check from my service pay to bury him."

"I'm sorry."

Heath shrugged. "Nothing to be sorry about, he'd been killing himself for years with the booze."

"It's an illness, Heath."

"It's a weakness. You'll never see me go that way."

"There are all different forms of weakness, Heath. Maybe your father's was just more obvious than some others."

"On the soapbox again? Don't defend him to me, you didn't know him."

"I saw enough of him that day to imagine what your childhood with him was like."

"Even your writer's imagination isn't that good," he said flatly, and Ann dropped the subject.

When Heath pulled into the circle in front of the Imperial Plaza two uniformed valets flew over to the car as if magnetized. The doors swung open and their minimal luggage vanished as the taller man said to Heath, "It's nice to see you again, Mr. Bodine. Will you be staying with us long?"

"A few days."

The valet glanced at Ann curiously as Heath said, "This is Mrs. Bodine."

"A pleasure to meet you, ma'am," the valet said as Ann tried to adjust to hearing herself introduced that way.

The second man returned from depositing their bags on the steps and looked into Ann's face for the first time as he closed her door.

"Miss Talbot?" he said in astonishment.

Ann paused for a moment and gazed back at him. He looked vaguely familiar.

"Yes?" she said.

"Don't you remember me? Carlos Sanchez, Luisa's nephew. I used to drop her off at work at your house sometimes."

"Oh, yes, Carlos. Of course. It's been a long time, hasn't it? How are you?"

"I'm fine. Though my Aunt Luisa died a few years ago."

"Yes, I know. I heard. I'm very sorry."

"Thanks. What are you doing back in the Keys? Nobody's seen you around here for the longest time."

"She came here to get married," Heath said, walking around the car and joining them. "Ann is my wife."

Carlos stared at Heath and then smiled slowly. "So you two got together, anyway," he said.

"Anyway?" Heath inquired.

"Aunt Luisa used to talk about how Henry Talbot was trying to break up your romance."

"With her expert assistance," Heath said humorlessly, staring at Carlos.

"Yeah, well, she was very devoted to Mr. Talbot," Carlos said, looking from one to the other nervously.

"Yes, she was," Ann said, shooting Heath a look. "And my father appreciated it very much. It was wonderful to see you again, Carlos, but it's been a long day and I'm very tired. Do you think we could go up to our room now?"

"Sure, sure," Carlos said, happy to extricate himself from what had quickly become an uncomfortable situation. He and the other valet preceded Heath and Ann up the wide stairs of the hotel and into the spacious, marble-floored lobby. It was tastefully decorated in Florida pastels and open to the air on all four sides behind floor-to-ceiling glass doors.

"Mr. Bodine!" the desk clerk said with a broad smile. "It's delightful to have you staying with us again. And this must be your wife. What a lovely lady, you have excellent taste. Mrs. Bodine, how do you do?"

Ann shook his hand and then watched as he bustled over to get the room key.

"These people all greet you like a long-lost relative," she said to Heath.

"I spend a lot of time in hotels," he replied shortly.

When they reached the suite, Carlos was already setting their bags on the luggage rest in the foyer. Heath tipped him and Carlos flashed Ann a smile and said, "Good to see you back in Florida, Miss Talbot—I mean, Mrs. Bodine."

Heath slammed the door shut behind him. "Still bowing and scraping before you, aren't they?" he said disgustedly.

"I don't know what you mean," Ann said.

"Of course you do. You can't resist playing lady of the manor with the underlings."

"I was just being polite to him, Heath. You should try it sometime."

"I seem to have done all right with my inadequate manners. We didn't have too many finishing schools in Hispaniola."

"Why do you have such a chip on your shoulder? What was I supposed to do, Heath, ignore him? I knew him years ago—his aunt worked for my family a long time."

"His aunt was your father's dupe! He thought of her as a convenience, somebody to wash his clothes and cook his food—a peasant from shantytown! She thought she was his friend, and she ceased to exist for him the moment he could no longer use her."

"That isn't true, Heath. My father left her enough money in his will to retire to a nice place in Miami. It wasn't his fault that she didn't live long enough to enjoy it."

"You're justifying your father's behavior to me now?" Heath said incredulously. They were standing in the suite's foyer, arguing like two barristers.

"I'm not defending him. I'm merely telling you that he repaid Luisa for her loyalty."

"King Henry doling out the royal favors," Heath said sarcastically.

"I have more reason to hate him than you do. I'm just trying to be fair."

"You're just acting like a princess born to the purple. It must be true what they say—it's in the blood."

"It's in the way you treat other people. You can't buy—" She stopped.

"What? Class, good breeding, refinement?" he said sneeringly. "Sure you can. I bought you, didn't I?"

Stung, Ann didn't reply for a second, then said, "You bought my body, Heath. That's all."

"That's enough." He tossed his jacket onto the foyer table and left the suite.

Ann sagged against the wall, drained as if she had just run a marathon. How could they go on like this? They had been married only a couple of hours and were already at each other's throats.

She walked desultorily into the parlor with its adjoining bedroom. The rooms were large and light, richly appointed and lushly carpeted, with a balcony overlooking the beach and an ornate bathroom. This was done in the same marble as the lobby floor, with a Jacuzzi tub and gilt fixtures. Ann paused in the doorway and looked around. His and her plush bathrobes hung on the back of the door and the vanity contained a tall glass jar filled with little soaps in the shapes of seashells. Everything was wrapped in paper, including the toilet. Stacks of thick towels filled the shelves next to the shower and a tray on the sink held miniature bottles of everything from herbal shampoo to mint hand lotion.

Ann had never stayed at the Imperial, but she knew it had been one of her father's favorites.

She went back into the bedroom and hung the few things she had brought with her in the capacious closet. She had no idea where Heath had gone or when he would be back, so she went to the phone and called her brother to see how he'd been doing, her editor in New York, and Amy Horton. She stretched the conversations out as long as she could. Then, depressed by the events of the day and bone weary from the stress of containing her emotions, she undressed to her camisole and briefs and lay down on the embroidered bedspread.

In minutes she was asleep.

Ann was conscious of nothing for the next several hours. When she came to, the room was dark and Heath was sitting next to her on the bed, his hand on her shoulder.

Ann knew it was Heath before she was even awake, before she remembered the wedding or their circumstances. She knew it instinctively, from his scent, his posture, the feel of his fingers. Without a word she turned into his arms.

Heath held her loosely for a moment and she put her head on his shoulder. Then his grip tightened and his mouth came down hard and fast on hers.

Ann's mind spun out, reeling back to the summer they had shared. The kiss he had given her at their wedding was light, fleeting, but this one recalled the passion of the two teenagers who had come together like a spark and tinder, never to be the same again.

In an instant Ann forgot the sarcastic remarks, the sullen looks, the fury and bitterness he had shown her since their reunion. She was seventeen, and this was Heath, whom she loved so much. Her lips opened to admit his probing tongue as his hands slipped under her camisole, seeking her skin. His fingers were still rough as a boy's, callused, and she shivered as he ran his hands up her bare arms and across her back, lifting the scrap of silk over her head and tossing it onto the floor. She gasped against his mouth as his hand closed over her breast and she felt his thumb rasp her nipple, increasing the pressure until she moaned and her head fell back, exposing an expanse of soft, pale skin.

He bent his head and ran his tongue along the slender line of her throat, holding her to him with one arm and lifting her legs with the other. He lay back on the bed, pulling her down with him, and she sighed as she felt him along the length of her, his mouth moving from the hollow between her breasts to each sensitive nipple, sucking gently. Ann held his head, his thick hair like strands of raw silk against her fingers, his lips caressing her until she tugged on him to raise his head. His long-lashed eyes looked down into hers in the dim room, his skin dusky against the collar of his crisp white shirt, his mouth wet and reddened from her kisses.

"I missed you so much," she whispered, reaching up to touch his still face, tracing his full lips tenderly with a forefinger. "Come back to me."

He obeyed, bending to press his burning cheek to her belly, slipping one hand under her hips to lift her as he pulled off her briefs with the other. She closed her eyes as his fingers slid over her thigh and then between her legs. She whimpered and bit her lip, inhaling sharply as his caresses brought her to an anxious pitch of arousal. When he moved back suddenly, she clutched his arms and found them knotted and rigid with tension. It was costing him something to make love to her in this practiced, disciplined way; he wanted—or feared—to lose control as much as she did.

That knowledge gave her hope and encouragement. She remembered how he had once responded to her slightest movement and she leaned forward, moving astride him. He was still dressed, but she felt him as if he were naked, powerful and ready between her thighs. His hands slipped down her back and cupped her buttocks, his lips compressed, his chest heaving. She bent forward and kissed his throat, moving her hand inside the waistband of his pants. She felt his abdominal muscles contract beneath her fingers, and he made a helpless, guttural sound. Seconds later he thrust her away from him almost roughly, as if afraid of revealing too much.

"Heath," she said, clinging to him.

For one awful moment she thought he was going to shrug her off and leave. But desire won, as it always had with them. He tore off his shirt and pants, stripping so quickly that she hardly had a glimpse of him in the scant light from the foyer before he joined her. He gently pushed her back to the bed and held her arms above her head and moved over her, kissing her wildly until she was wrapping her bare legs around his hips, reaching for him and pressing against him intimately.

He kissed her body feverishly, his awareness of his own strength diminished as he finally drove into her wildly, all control gone, making her cry out with the sensation. When he paused, thinking he had hurt her, she dug her nails into his hips and urged him onward, pressing her heels into the backs of his legs. He surged into her repeatedly, catching her up in his rhythm, his back slick with sweat so her hands slipped along it, his hair at his nape damp and clinging to her fingers. He lowered his head and pressed his face into the soft, warm curve of her shoulder. Everything about him was beloved to her, and well remembered: the yielding softness of his mouth, the hardness of his body, the effortless sureness of his movements. Tears seeped from under Ann's closed lids as he quickened his pace, carrying her along with him.

Heath, she thought desperately. *Heath, I still love you so much.* She bit her lip as she spiraled upward, moaning with him in mutual release. Then she could feel their hearts pounding together as he relaxed against her, the beat slowing as she stroked his hair and ran her fingers down the length of his spine. When he moved, she turned to embrace him, then fell back against the bed in shock as he released her abruptly and stood, walking to the bathroom without a word.

She lay still and listened to the start of the shower beyond the connecting wall, then listened again as he emerged in a cloud of steam and soap scent, to dress in the dark.

It wasn't until she heard the door click closed behind him that she really believed he was gone.

He had used her like a whore, taking his pleasure and then washing off her smell and touch, the memory of their lovemaking sluicing off in a rush of steam and suds.

He clearly thought of them like two striped cats coupling in an alley.

Ann turned her face into the pillow and cried.

Chapter 8

Ann spent a week at the Imperial Plaza with Heath and then they moved back to his house on Lime Island. The housekeeper and her husband had returned. They were polite but distant; Heath's marriage had been a surprise and they were taking their time to make a judgment about their new mistress.

Ann filled her days working on her book, visiting with Tim and conferring with his lawyers about his case, and planning the annual Christmas party Heath gave for his executives. In the past, his office had handled the event, but this year Heath wanted his wife to act as hostess. Ann knew that her involvement was part of his trophy-wife syndrome but she went along with it as she had gone along with everything else, considering it part of her bargain. The task kept her busy as Christmas approached, and she was glad of the distraction; she didn't feel much like cel-

ebrating the holidays this year and Heath was often
gone on business. She was lonely in the big house,
looking forward to his returns in spite of her misgiv-
ings about their arrangement.

At least when he was home he slept with her.

In bed, he was passionate, demanding, fulfilling,
everything she could have wanted. Out of bed he
treated her like a doorstop, a convenience to be noticed only when needed.

Ann wasn't very happy.

The party was scheduled for the day before Christmas Eve, and that morning Ann oversaw the florist's
delivery, watching as the house was transformed into
a holiday bower. The rooms were banked with poin-
settias and a large, decorated spruce was set up in the
entry hall, ready to greet the guests as they arrived. At
four, the food service arrived, and Ann checked off
the items with the caterer as trucks disgorged folding
tables and napery and silver. The uniformed waiters
would come later, along with the liquor and the
glassware and the entertainment. By seven o'clock,
Heath was still not home, Daniela and Victor were
hard at work with the caterers, and there was nothing for Ann to do but get dressed.

The radio blared Christmas carols as Ann bathed
and dressed in what she still thought of as Heath's
bedroom. Heath was generous with money, if not
with himself, and Ann just charged anything she
wanted, discovering quickly that she didn't want
much. Heath had told her to buy an outfit for this
occasion and she had settled on an evening pantsuit
of blond silk, with a tunic top embroidered at the
sleeve cuffs with gold sequins. It was elegant and un-
derstated, just what she wanted. She was fixing gold

studs to her ears when the intercom buzzed. Ann leaned over to flick the switch and said, "What is it?"

"You have a visitor, Mrs. Bodine," Daniela's voice replied.

"Now? Who is it?"

"A Miss Horton."

"Amy? For heaven's sake, send her in!"

Seconds later Amy burst through the door, her arms loaded with gaily wrapped packages, her face split by a huge grin.

"Surprise!" she said, and threw her bundles in a colored jumble onto the bed.

Ann hugged her friend and said, "Am I glad to see you! I'm facing this shindig tonight and I could sure use an ally. But I thought you weren't coming."

"I changed my mind. I broke up with Graham and I found myself with a free night, thought you wouldn't mind if I just sort of turned up for the festivities."

"How could I mind, you're a lifesaver. You'll be the only person at this party not connected to Heath's business, which is reason enough to welcome you with open arms."

"It looks like they're cooking up quite a soiree out there. The house looks beautiful, and so do you."

"Thanks."

"Where is Himself?"

"Not home yet."

Amy sat on the edge of the bed and unbuttoned the light sweater she was wearing. "How is it going with him?"

A shadow crossed Ann's face and she shook her head without comment.

"But you love him, don't you?" Amy asked.

Ann looked away, then nodded.

"Any hope?"

"I doubt it. He's just going to play this revenge game until he gets tired of me, but I think I can keep it going long enough to at least get Tim out of trouble. Heath enjoys displaying me as his wife, having me act as his hostess—Henry Talbot's daughter on the arm of the self-made man. That's very important to him, but I'm sure the novelty of it will pale with time."

"Then what happens to you?"

"I get discarded, like the first wives of most millionaires who move on, I suppose."

"It sounds like a raw deal for you."

"It's not so bad, except..."

"Except what?"

"Except that I do love him," Ann said, biting her lip, her eyes stinging with tears. "It's so hard being around him all the time, having him look through me as if I were a pane of glass. He gives me everything, just not what I really want. Him."

"How's the sex?"

Ann smiled wanly. "Come on, Amy. You know that's not the problem."

"I didn't think it was. So, what's the plan? What are you going to do?"

"Stick it out. I have no choice."

"Well, for tonight at least, I'm here to help you. I brought along a nifty little dress that should liven things up quite a bit once I slip into it. What time are the guests arriving?"

"Eight."

"I'd better step lively then. Where's the john?"

Ann pointed and Amy disappeared inside the bathroom, emerging ten minutes later in a spangled black mini sheath and *peau de soie* T-strap shoes.

"What do you think?" she said to Amy, posing with one hand on her hip.

"You're a showstopper."

"Exactly the effect I'm trying to achieve. Darling, I hate to be a bore, but I drove three hours to get here and I'm starving. Do you think I could slip into the kitchen for a little something? Otherwise I will be drinking on an empty stomach, which is never a good idea in my case. They never serve anything to eat at these things until everybody is plastered."

"Go ahead. I'll call Daniela and tell her to make you a sandwich, okay?"

"Okay."

Amy had just left when Heath walked into the bedroom, putting down his briefcase and pulling his tie loose from its knot. He surveyed her in silence.

"Is this outfit all right?" Ann inquired, indicating her new clothes.

"Fine."

"How does the house look?"

"Looks good."

"Did you see the buffet table?"

"I saw it."

Ann gave up. "Amy is here," she said resignedly.

"I saw her in the kitchen on the way in. I didn't know that you had invited her."

"Do you mind?"

He shrugged.

"She's not an employee of Bimini Boat Works," Ann said dryly, fastening a gold bracelet around her wrist.

"I never said that you couldn't have your friends here," he replied, taking off his jacket.

"No, Heath, you never said that," Ann agreed, running a brush through her hair.

He turned and faced her. "You really think I'm a bully, don't you?" he said quietly.

Ann didn't answer.

He unbuttoned his shirt and tossed it onto the bed. "I'm not a bully, Princess. I just have a long memory." He went into the bathroom and turned on the shower.

Ann heard the doorbell and realized that the first guests were arriving. She put down the hairbrush and went out of the bedroom to fulfill her role.

Several hours later, she was in the kitchen slicing a lemon when Amy sidled in behind her.

"Isn't the caterer supposed to do that?" Amy asked.

"They ran out of lemons."

"The party is a smash. You're a hit."

Ann nodded.

"You don't seem very happy about it."

Out on the terrace, the three-piece band switched from "Winter Wonderland" to "White Christmas."

"No word from your lord and master about what a wonderful job you did?" Amy said.

"No."

"He's a jerk, Ann."

"I guess he just regards my doing this as part of our deal. I didn't actually cook the food or serve it, anyway. I just hired a bunch of people."

"You've got—what, a hundred people out there? Just coordinating the whole event was a task. Doesn't he know you were trying to please him?"

"I can't imagine what he thinks. His mind is a closed book." She sighed. "I used to know him so well."

"Well, one thing hasn't changed. He's still the most gorgeous man I've ever seen. He makes every other guy at this party look three days dead."

"That aspect of it doesn't exactly help, Amy. It only makes me want him more, and he's very good at keeping me at a comfortable distance."

"Comfortable for him."

"Yes."

"Working all the time?" Amy said.

"Yes."

"Noncommittal when he's at home?"

"You got it."

"He sounds just like your father."

Ann shuddered. "That would be the supreme irony, wouldn't it?" she said sadly.

The sliding door to the terrace opened and Joan Jensen stepped through it.

"Hi, sweetie," she said to Ann, and smiled at Amy. "Everybody is having a great time, including my husband. He doesn't quite have a lampshade on his head yet, but he's getting there."

"I'll just go check on those canapés," Amy said, raising her brows, and Ann nodded. Amy slipped out of the room.

"Heath must be very pleased," Joan said brightly.

"I imagine so."

"He hasn't said anything?"

"Well, he's been very busy. He's the host, after all. I've hardly seen him."

Joan looked around quickly and then stepped into the hall, scanning the immediate area. Then she rejoined Ann, leaning in close to her and saying, "What's going on, Ann?"

Ann looked at her.

"Don't give me that innocent face," Joan said kindly. "I've been watching you and Heath for almost a month. You're both drawn, tense and unhappy. You look thinner every day and Heath is snapping at Joe if my husband looks at him cross-eyed. You're not exactly the picture of blissful newlyweds. What gives?"

Ann looked away from her.

"I thought something was wrong at your wedding, but Joe dismissed it. Now even he is beginning to wonder. Why did you marry Heath, Ann?"

Ann sighed wearily. "You remember us when we were kids, right, Joan?"

"How could I forget? I never saw two people more in love. Joe and I were just thrilled when the two of you got back together, that's why I can't understand this situation now. You've been given a second chance, why aren't you taking advantage of it?"

"It's a long story. What has Heath told you?"

"Nothing. He just called Joe one day and asked us to witness your wedding."

"Then let's keep it that way."

Joan stood aside as Ann slid the tray of lemons into the refrigerator. When Ann turned back to her, the older woman was watching her with concern.

Ann smiled. "I'm all right, Joan. Really."

Joan shook her head. She was a little plumper, a little grayer, than when Ann had first met her so many years ago, but her air of enveloping kindness was the same.

"I don't know if this helps you, but Heath really does have a good heart," Joan said.

Ann nodded.

"I mean it. The first thing he did when he came into that money was call Joe and offer him a job in management in the company he was forming. Management! Joe never even graduated from high school. And when Joe couldn't sell the marina—it was the middle of the recession, you know—Heath bought it himself, at a loss. He's been a wonderful friend to us, Ann."

"Heath was always grateful that Joe gave him a job when he needed one," Ann murmured.

"He's very loyal."

To everyone except me, Ann thought.

As if he had been summoned, Joe appeared and said, "What are you two hens clucking about in here? Everybody is dancing out on the terrace."

"I'm coming," Joan said, and put her hand on Ann's arm. "If you ever need to talk..." she said in a low tone.

Ann nodded. She waited until the Jensens had left and then walked around to the front of the house, nodding at the people she encountered along the way. The party was concentrated at the back of the house and she found herself alone at the front door, the sounds of music and laughter drifting toward her faintly through the rooms.

Ann opened the door and walked out onto the flagstone path, wrapping her arms around her torso. The night was cool for December in south Florida, in the high fifties, but it felt refreshing by comparison with the house, which was warm from collected body heat. Ann looked at the lights Victor had strung in the trees, the floodlit wreath hanging under the point of the garage roof, then gazed up at the stars, thinking about Christmases from her childhood. It was a minute or so before she realized that she was not alone.

She turned to find a young woman standing behind her, smoking a cigarette.

"So you're the wife, huh?" the smoker said.

"I . . . uh, yes," Ann replied, startled.

The woman switched her cigarette to her left hand and extended her right hand. "Stacy Barcroft," she said.

"How do you do?" Ann said, shaking hands with her.

"I'm doing just fine. I just came out here to grab a smoke. I didn't see any ashtrays inside so I figured I'd better not light up in the house."

"There are ashtrays in the pool room."

"Segregating the smokers, huh? That's okay, I'm used to it. We're the new persecuted minority. Actually, I don't mind going outside, it gives me a chance to catch a breath of air. It's getting pretty close in there."

"I just told Victor to turn on the air-freshening system in the house."

"Good idea." Stacy inhaled deeply, the tip of her cigarette glowing, then exhaled a plume of grayish smoke that danced on the cool night air. She stepped into the light from the windows and Ann saw that she was a petite brunette wearing a stylish red evening suit with black velvet trim.

"Do you work for Bimini in Miami?" Ann asked. "I remember your name from the guest list."

"No, I'm an architect. I designed the Miami marina, and I have been called in on a few other independent projects. I also dated Heath for a while."

"Oh."

"Don't get nervous, I gave up on him real quick. His body was present but it was clear his mind was always elsewhere, you know what I mean?"

Ann didn't reply. She knew.

"So you arrived out of the past, right? High school sweetheart or something like that?"

"Something like that."

"I suppose you know that women have been jumping off buildings all over south Florida since the day you got married."

Ann smiled thinly. "No, I didn't know that."

"It's a fact. Mr. Eligible decamps with a mystery woman from his student days? It caused quite a stir."

"It's already yesterday's news."

"Don't count on it. I'll bet you didn't get many regrets in response to your invitations to this party."

"That's true."

"And you thought everybody was showing up because Heath was the boss?"

"Yes, of course."

"Maybe. But they also wanted to see you."

Ann sighed. "I hope I wasn't a disappointment."

"How could you be? A tall, slim blonde with cover girl cheekbones? The minute I set my eyes on you, all my questions were answered."

"Really?" Ann said frostily, studying her companion. She was beginning to dislike this conversation intensely. If this woman had an ax to grind she was going to find herself alone out here with the Christmas lights.

Stacy waved her cigarette. "Don't get your nose out of joint. I only meant that I understand what he sees in you. I come from a background like Heath's. I came up from nothing, like him. I married my ex-husband, Jamie Barcroft, because he was born in Greenwich and went to Exeter and Yale. Heath and I both crave class, and people like you are the closest we're ever going to come to it."

"Thank you for your analysis of my marriage. I think I'd better get back inside and look after my guests."

Stacy put her hand on Ann's arm. "I'm sorry if I offended you. Maybe there are some sour grapes in what I'm saying, but it's also true. Just a word to the wise, that's all."

"Thank you. Good night."

"Merry Christmas," Stacy said, turning away as Ann opened the door to the house.

Inside, the first few leave-takers were getting ready to depart. Ann spent the next hour shaking hands and saying goodbye, her feet and her head beginning to ache. She barely saw Heath, who always seemed to be off in some corner deep in conversation with one of his executives. Finally she abandoned her post by the door and went up to the bedroom to get a glass of water to take some aspirin.

In the bedroom she found a man she had met twice that night and whose name she could not recall—the manager of the Bimini repair garage on Big Palm. She had danced with him earlier in the evening. He looked up as she arrived. He grinned sheepishly.

"Hi, Mrs. Bodine. I was just getting my raincoat, but there's a pile here on the bed and I can't find it."

"Oh, please, let me help you. I'm so sorry, I've forgotten your name."

"Ben Rowell."

"I can't believe so many coats wound up in here. I thought there was enough room in the front hall closet, but I guess I was wrong. What color is it?"

"Kind of an olive green—here it is," Ben said triumphantly. As he turned to smile at Ann she felt the room spin and she reached out instinctively, clutching him to maintain her balance. He pulled her into his arms to keep her from sliding to the floor.

At the same instant Heath came rushing through the door, grabbed Ben by the shoulder to pull him off Ann, and then punched the other man squarely in the jaw.

Ben staggered back in shock, staring at Heath, his eyes wide with amazement and dismay. Ann was rooted, gaping in disbelief at her husband, who seemed to have lost his mind.

"What the hell do you think you're doing with my wife?" Heath shouted, lunging for Ben again. Ann recovered enough to jump in front of Heath and block his path to the other man.

"Stop it this instant!" she snapped at Heath. "I felt a little dizzy and Ben was only trying to help me!"

"Why did you come back here to the bedroom with him?" Heath demanded, his eyes blazing.

"For heaven's sake, Heath, I didn't come back here with him. I found him in here looking for his coat. Will you calm down and apologize? You're making a fool of yourself."

"I saw him looking at you all night," Heath insisted, taking a step forward again.

Joe Jensen arrived, drawn by the sound of raised voices, and Ann was never so glad to see anyone in her life.

"What's going on here?" Joe demanded, looking around at the three of them.

"Ben was helping me when I felt faint and Heath misunderstood the situation," Ann said quickly. "Will you take him outside for a walk, Joe? I think he's had too much to drink."

"I'm perfectly sober—enough to see what was going on right under my nose," Heath said belligerently.

Joe gripped him firmly by the arm and steered him into the hall, as Ann went to Ben and took his hand.

"I'm so sorry about this, Ben. My only explantion is that Heath has been under a strain, working very hard, and I think he just had one too many tonight."

"It's all right, Mrs. Bodine. Everybody gets a snootful now and then, there's no harm done. Just the same, I think I'd better go. I'll say good-night now."

Ann saw him out the door with extreme relief and then came upon Joe and Heath in the living room, where Joe was giving her husband a lecture, talking earnestly to Heath's bent dark head.

"I'm telling you right now, boy, you'd better get hold of yourself and straighten up quickly. That little girl is going to leave you in the dust just as fast as she married you if you keep acting this way. You're just lucky that everybody but Joanie and me was outside or you would have put on quite a performance for a whole houseful of your employees."

Heath didn't move.

"And first thing tomorrow morning," Joe went on, "you get your tail over to Big Palm and apologize to that kid Ben. A few more incidents like this and you'll get a reputation as a crazy man who can't hold his liquor. What do you think that will do for your business, not to mention your personal life? These islands are small, word travels fast. And I don't have to tell you that you owe your wife an apology, too."

Heath was listening sullenly, his eyes on the floor. Joe looked up and saw Ann standing there.

"I'll leave you two alone. Joanie and I will see ourselves out."

Joe walked past Ann, patting her arm on the way. Ann went to the wall intercom, flipped the switch, and said into it, "Daniela, you and Victor can go to bed now. We'll deal with whatever mess the caterers leave behind in the morning."

"Don't you want me to just run the vacuum, Mrs. Bodine?" Daniela asked.

"Never mind, there will be time enough tomorrow."

"Mrs. Bodine," Daniela said. "Your friend Amy left about half an hour ago. She asked me to tell you she was staying at the inn and would call you in the morning."

"Thank you, Daniela. You did a wonderful job and Mr. Bodine and I are very grateful for your help. Good night."

"Good night," Daniela said, and Ann flicked the switch to the Off position.

Heath was still standing in the same spot, careful not to look at her.

"The party was a great success," Ann said. "You should give Daniela and Victor a bonus."

"And what should I give you? You planned it."

"I assumed that it was part of my job."

"And was flirting with Ben Rowell part of your job?"

Ann sighed and turned away. "Heath, you are deranged. I wound up with him in the bedroom at the same time by accident. He was looking for his coat."

"He was looking for more than that."

"Heath, I am not going to spar with you, especially on this ludicrous subject. It's been a long evening and I am very tired. I'm going to bed."

"Not so fast," he snapped, covering the distance between them in two long strides. He grabbed her arm and she was unable to take another step.

"Heath, you're hurting me," she said, twisting uselessly in his grasp.

"Do you think I'm blind? I saw you dancing with Ben earlier tonight. I saw the way he was holding you, talking to you. You seemed to be enjoying yourself very much."

"He was telling me funny stories about the grand opening of the Big Palm marina, about everything that went wrong that day. I was just trying to be a good hostess, Heath. If you had half a brain in your head you'd realize that the man wouldn't endanger his job by courting the boss's wife in front of the rest of the company. What the devil is wrong with you?"

"And who asked if you were hungry? Who ran to get you a plate?" Heath demanded, ignoring the logic of her last statement.

"Ben was just being polite. If it were up to you I would have starved! Has it occurred to you that just maybe he felt sorry for me? My husband ignored me all evening to conduct momentous business conversations that should have taken place in the office. At least, I thought you were ignoring me. Obviously you were keeping track of me by radar, watching my tiniest move while pretending to be absorbed in weighty discussion." She finally yanked her arm free and stood rubbing her wrist, glaring at him.

"I was admiring your act," he said.

"What act?"

"Your dutiful wife and hostess act. I must say that it was very entertaining."

"I wasn't acting, Heath. I intend to fulfill my part of our bargain completely."

"No matter how much it hurts, huh?"

Ann didn't answer.

"You think I don't know what's been going through your head?" Heath said. "You've been feeling sorry for yourself. Poor Annie, ignored by an indifferent husband, all your charms wasted on a brute who couldn't possibly appreciate them. Then tonight you saw a chance for real admiration from that boy and you couldn't resist it."

"I'm not that shallow, Heath," Ann said quietly.

"Of course not. You're the Ice Princess—ideal wife, arm adornment and party planner. I knew this evening would be perfect, you learned to entertain at your momma's knee. Too bad she didn't teach you about fidelity."

"I'm not going to listen to any more of this," Ann said, starting for the bedroom again.

He blocked her path. "You enjoy teasing me, don't you? Making me imagine what you might be up to with a guy like that? It's the only way you have of getting back at me—isn't it?—letting me picture somebody else kissing you, touching you, holding you?" His eyes were wild, his face flushed, his fists clenched.

His attack was so baseless and unfair, and Ann was so exhausted, that she had finally had enough. Her patience ran out and she said icily, "You know, you really shouldn't drink, Heath, not with your family history. A couple of more belts and you could permanently turn into your father."

His hand came up like lightning and Ann faced him down regally, her gaze direct and unflinching.

"Go ahead and hit me, Heath. You've been wanting to hit me for eleven years. Maybe if you finally get it out of your system you'll feel better."

His hand faltered, then fell. He looked at her a long moment, then dashed headlong from the room. Ann heard the door to the garage slam and then the sound of his car starting. She listened as it roared into the street and then faded into the distance.

In the kitchen, Daniela had left the radio on the counter playing softly. In the new silence, the strains of "Have Yourself A Merry Little Christmas" drifted into the living room.

Ann sat wearily on the sofa, too numb to cry.

Heath drove in circles for half an hour before deciding on his destination—an all-night bar by the railroad tracks at the edge of Hispaniola. The plastic Christmas decorations on the door and the colored lights strung along the bar did nothing to lift his spirits as he slid onto a stool and ordered a drink he didn't really want. When it came, he pushed it back and forth without touching it, watching the trail of moisture it left on the scarred wood of the bar.

Why had he behaved that way tonight? He couldn't seem to stop punishing Ann, no matter how stoic she was about enduring his moods. He was proud of her, but couldn't admit it; he admired her, but couldn't say it. In fact, the more impeccably she filled her role as his wife the more enraged he felt. His need to make her pay was bottomless. She had done exactly what she'd promised to do before their marriage, and his inability to find fault with her made him want to kick in the walls. Why? Because she had to be a fraud, she had to be fickle and flighty and faithless, or else he had wasted more than a decade of his life hating a person who didn't remotely deserve it.

Somebody put "Jingle Bells" on the jukebox and Heath tried to block out the sound; holiday music only depressed him further. He had felt like an actor, playing his role at the party tonight, all the while conscious that he didn't deserve Ann or the dedication she had shown in making the event a success. He knew he was rude and unfeeling and charmless toward her. He also knew that he wanted nothing more than to hold her in his arms all night long and tell her everything he was feeling, everything he had kept bottled up inside for years like champagne canted under pressure. But that would be folly, wouldn't it? If she knew that his pretense of emotional indifference was becoming impossible to sustain, that he almost didn't care anymore what she had done in the past or why, then she would win.

But was winning this contest—his unbending attitude versus her ability to endure it—really that important to him anymore? If he were honest with himself, he would have to admit that keeping her with him was fast becoming the major—possibly the only—consideration. Every time he thought of the way she turned to him so trustingly in bed, gave of herself so completely in spite of his churlish behavior, his will to continue the vendetta ebbed a little more.

Heath hadn't noticed that the stool next to his was now occupied until his neighbor said to him, "Coming from a big date?"

Heath looked down at the tuxedo he'd forgotten he was wearing. "I guess you could say that."

"How'd it go?"

Heath ran his finger around the rim of his whiskey glass. "Not well," he replied.

"That's a shame. Seems to me like everyone tries too hard at this time of the year, like we're all forcing ourselves to be happy, even if we're not."

Heath glanced at the philosopher to his left and narrowed his eyes. The old man looked familiar.

"Don't I know you?" Heath asked.

The man nodded. "You should. I picked you up about five times in my squad car, as I recall. Heath Bodine, isn't it?"

"It sure is," Heath said, extending his hand. "Refresh my memory. You are...?"

"Ken Gates. Sergeant, Lime Island police force. Retired." He shook Heath's hand.

Heath grinned. "Sure, I remember. We used to call you Gatecrasher. How the hell are you?"

"Just great. I'm down here from Chicago to visit my son for the holidays."

"So why are you here at this bar?"

"I had to get away from the grandchildren."

Heath laughed. "At two in the morning?"

"The baby woke up for a feeding, and so we all did. That kid has lungs she inherited from my late wife, may God rest her soul." He downed the rest of his drink. "So, what are you doing in this dive, kid? I heard you made a mint on some boat gizmo you invented a few years ago and bought the old Curtis spread. Isn't this place a little lowlife for you these days?"

"I feel right at home," Heath said in a tired voice.

"Not drinking?" Gates asked, nodding toward Heath's full glass of Scotch.

"I've already had enough tonight."

"Afraid of winding up like your old man?"

"The thought has crossed my mind."

"I had him in the drunk tank more than once."

"I'm sure you did."

"He was harmless, kid."

"He was worthless."

"Is that why you're sitting here with a bunch of strangers two days before Christmas?"

"I had a fight with my wife."

"Ahh. What did she do?"

"Nothing. It was my fault."

"Did you tell her that?"

"No."

"Then I guess I can see why you're here."

Gates signaled for another drink and Heath said, "I got it." When the bartender arrived, Heath said, "Keep them coming for my man here. On my tab."

The bartender nodded and walked away to get Gates another whiskey.

"Thanks, kid. I guess you can afford it. It's funny, I never would have pegged you for a future success story."

"You weren't the only one."

"Did you marry a local girl?"

"She used to be local. Henry Talbot's girl. Do you remember her?"

"I hope to say I do. Pretty as a picture—blond hair, big blue eyes. Didn't you have a thing going with her a few years ago?"

"More than a few. How did you know that?"

"Old Henry was down at the station one night at the end of one summer, must have been about ten years ago, trying to get us to arrest you for statutory rape with that little girl."

Heath froze with his hand around the glass on the bar before him. "What?" he said softly.

Gates nodded vigorously. "I remember it like it was yesterday. We didn't see much of the local gentry in the squad room, if you know what I mean, so the incident kind of stuck in my mind. Talbot wanted to know the procedure necessary for filing charges. The chief tried to talk him out of it—we all guessed it was probably just a case of two kids in love. The Talbot girl was only a few months away from the legal age anyway, right? But King Henry was having none of it. He left determined to file the charges as soon as he squeezed the necessary details out of his kid. Then, like magic, we heard nothing more about it. A few weeks later, the Talbot housekeeper told me that the girl had gone up north to school, and later I read in the paper that you had joined the navy. I figured then that the girl had agreed to leave town if her daddy let you off the hook."

Heath was staring at him, his fingers white around the object he held, his breath caught in his throat.

"You all right, kid?" Gates asked, concerned. "You look kinda... funny."

Heath stood slowly, sliding off his stool and pulling a bill out of his wallet. He set it down on the bar.

"This should cover everything," he said, then clapped Gates on the shoulder and reached once more for his hand.

"Thank you," Heath said soberly. "And merry Christmas. And happy New Year."

Gates shook his hand, stared after him for a moment, then snatched up the bill and tucked it into his pocket, signaling the bartender.

Ann was asleep on the sofa in the living room when Heath returned. He took off his shoes and crept closer to the couch, noting with dismay that even in sleep her brow was creased and her expression not peaceful. Feeling guilty and remorseful to the limit of his imagination, Heath sat next to her and took her by the shoulders, gently lifting her into his arms. He remembered with a pang how he had found her in similar circumstances the day of their wedding. The deliberate cruelty of taking off and leaving her without a word on that occasion was unforgivable in retrospect, and he wondered now if their relationship was even salvageable.

He carried her into the bedroom and set her on the bed, leaning forward until she slipped bonelessly onto the embroidered spread. He took off her shoes and adjusted the pillow under her head, drawing an afghan over her legs as she stirred slightly. Then he crept quietly out of the room and closed the door.

He stood in the hallway for a long time, then went into the living room and sat staring out the windows at the lawn until the sky lightened and the sun rose.

When Joe Jensen came into his office around noon on Christmas Eve, Heath was sitting at his desk.

Joe stopped short. "What are you doing here?" he asked Heath in surprise.

"I called your house and Joan said you were coming in at lunchtime to pick up the mail."

"And you've just been sitting here waiting?"

"Yes."

Joe pulled out a chair and sat facing Heath. "What's up? As if I didn't know."

"I've already talked to Ben Rowell and apologized for last night," Heath said.

Joe nodded. "And your wife?"

"I haven't talked to her yet."

"What happened after Joan and I went home?"

"We had a fight and I left. When I came back, Ann was sleeping, and then I left again this morning before she was up."

"Are you avoiding her?"

Heath sighed. "I wish I could avoid myself," he said, running his hands through his hair.

Joe sat back with his arms folded, surveying Heath skeptically. "Kid, I haven't wanted to ask—"

Heath held up his hand. "And I haven't wanted to talk about it. Until now."

Joe shrugged. "Then go ahead."

Heath filled Joe in on the parts of the story he didn't know—the circumstances of the breakup with Ann when they were kids, how he had misjudged the situation and how he'd only married her for revenge.

Joe was staring at him in amazement when he finished.

"Do you mean to tell me that all these years you thought she dumped you until that old cop set you straight?"

"Yes."

"Even when she told you otherwise?"

Heath nodded wearily.

"I guess you had a whole lot of faith in her, didn't you?" Joe said dryly.

Heath said nothing.

"So what are you going to do now, start interviewing retired municipal staff and going through old police reports to make sure that Gates gave you the straight story?"

"No," Heath said quietly. "I believe him."

"But you didn't believe Ann when she told you the same thing," Joe observed mercilessly.

Heath just shook his head, his expression defeated.

"What are you going to do?" Joe asked, finally taking pity on his friend.

"I don't know. How can I ask her to forgive me for a mistake this enormous? The situation is impossible. You don't know how I've been treating her...."

"From your performance last night, I can guess."

"I married her to punish her," Heath said, rising abruptly. "And I did punish her, every way I could. Now it turns out she didn't deserve it at all. I feel like hiding out somewhere. Joe, I'm too ashamed to face her."

"Would you have kept treating her badly if you hadn't run into Gates?" Joe asked.

Heath shook his head slowly. "I doubt it. The whole act was becoming real hard to sustain."

"Act?"

"I don't hate her, Joe," Heath said softly, a catch in his voice. "I never did, even when I was trying to convince myself otherwise."

Joe nodded silently, moved by Heath's struggle to contain his emotions.

Heath put his head back against the wall and closed his eyes. "I don't know what to do," he said.

Joe waited, unsure what to say. In his experience, Heath had always known what to do.

Heath opened his eyes. "Any advice?" he said.

"Do you want her to stay with you?" Joe asked.

"Of course, but I can't keep holding her brother's fate over her head to coerce her."

"You don't think she'll stay with you otherwise?"

Heath was silent.

"Does she love you?"

"She did, but..."

Joe raised an eyebrow.

"I've done everything I could to destroy her affection for me. If it's survived, it will be a miracle."

"I'd bet she's a lot tougher than she looks," Joe said.

Heath nodded thoughtfully. "I've learned that during the past month."

"Then tell her what you're feeling. Don't give up now when you're so close to getting what you want."

"I don't know how close I am. She would never have married me in the first place if Tim weren't on his way to jail."

"That may have been the excuse she gave herself, but I'm sure she wanted to be with you, Heath. I remember when you were kids. I've never seen two people more in love."

"A lot of time has passed since then."

"Have your feelings changed?"

Heath didn't answer for a long time, then he shook his head once, unable to meet Joe's eyes.

"Chances are she feels the same. Go home and talk to her, Heath. I'm betting she'll listen."

Heath got up and walked toward the door, pausing as he passed Joe to put his hand on the older man's shoulder.

"Thanks, Joe," he said huskily.

Joe smiled to himself as the door closed behind Heath.

Heath drove back home in a fog of apprehension; he knew that he had to confront Ann about this now, since there was no possibility of going on as before, but he dreaded her reaction.

She had every right to throw him out of the house or leave him on the spot. The only mystery was why she hadn't done so already. But the idea that she might reject him now, after all that they had been through, was truly too awful to consider.

Ann was in the den, wrapping a Christmas present, when he arrived.

"Princess," he said softly from the doorway.

Her head shot up and she looked at him. Her expression cut him to the quick; she looked as if she were anticipating a blow. And why not? He had been delivering little else lately.

"Heath," she said, putting aside the gift. "I didn't know where you were."

"I came back last night but left again before you woke up this morning."

"I didn't expect you to come back."

He nodded dismally. "How are you feeling?"

"All right." She seemed surprised that he had asked.

"You said you were dizzy last night."

She appeared confused. "But I thought that you didn't believe me."

Heath leaned against the doorway and closed his eyes. "I believe you, Ann. I think some part of me always has. Are you sure that you're feeling better now?"

She nodded, clearly bewildered by his solicitous attitude. "I was too nervous to eat all day before the party, that's all. I wanted the evening to go well."

"It did go well, until I blew it at the end with my big mouth, of course."

"Nobody heard that, Heath. Nobody but Joe, and he's not going to say anything."

He stared at her in amazement. She was still worried about him, even though he didn't deserve it.

"Princess, I'm sorry," he said.

"It's all right, Heath. Forget it. I guess we were both tense last night. It's over now."

"I'm not talking about the incident with Ben Rowell. I'm talking about the way I've acted since we met again last month—the way I blackmailed you into marrying me and have used your brother's situation to keep you with me ever since."

Ann was so stunned she couldn't reply.

"I knew that I couldn't keep this charade going much longer. I think these irrational outbursts, like the one last night, were just reflections of my confusion."

"What charade?" Ann said softly.

"Pretending that I didn't care about you, that my only goal was to use you in bed and extract revenge for the past."

"You convinced me."

"I know. I've been a brute to you. Just thinking about some of the things I've said and done makes me cringe."

Ann stared at him for a moment, then said, "Why this change of heart now, Heath?"

He sighed, not surprised that she didn't know how to respond to this turnabout in his attitude.

"Ann, I know that the story you told me about your father prosecuting me for rape is true. Last night I talked to a cop who was on the Lime Island police force when your father was inquiring about assembling a case against me."

Her lips parted and he held up his hand. She waited breathlessly, watching him.

"I want you to understand that even before I spoke to him I knew that we couldn't go on like this. Torturing you wasn't as much fun as I'd thought it would be. In fact, it wasn't fun at all." He ran his hand through his disordered hair, then added, "I'm letting you out of the deal. You're free to go whenever you want and I'll make you a generous settlement. And as far as your brother goes, I'll continue to do everything I said I would, with no strings attached. He'll stay out of jail and I'll pay the attorneys for his trial. I've already bought up the stock in ScriptSoft and I'll oversee the company's recovery." He expelled his breath in a rush. "I guess that's all I have to say."

Ann swallowed hard, her expression unreadable, her body motionless.

"I'm going to leave for a couple of hours so you can make up your mind whether you want to stay here or return to New York. I'll clear out if you want the house until the divorce is settled. I'm sorry about the timing of this, Christmas and all, but it couldn't wait. I'll be back around three. You can let me know what you want to do then. I know I'm springing this on you suddenly, but is that enough time for you to decide? I just want to get this over with, not prolong the agony."

Ann nodded wordlessly.

Heath walked out of the den and Ann heard him leave.

She put her head down on her cradled arms and slowly closed her eyes.

The afternoon of Christmas Eve was the longest period of Heath's life. He had no idea what to do with himself, so he drove to the mall on Big Palm and sat on one of the stone benches, watching the tardy shoppers hurry by, the kids hysterical with pre-Christmas excitement and the parents rushed and preoccupied. He was oblivious to the Christmas carols blaring over the intercom and the advertisements for the last-minute sales while his whole history with Ann played itself over in his mind like a newsreel. He had surely blown his last chance with her, and that knowledge made him want to beg her to stay with him. But some warning instinct told him that she had to bring up that possibility herself.

He was through trying to force her into his mold. The idea must be hers.

When he got back to the house, the sun was beginning to decline in the winter sky and he found Ann sitting in the living room, waiting for him. She was dressed exactly as she had been when he'd left, and there were no bags in the hall.

Ann's eyes flooded with tears when she saw him.

He stared back at her, a muscle jumping along his jaw.

"Come here," she said.

Heath sat next to her on the loveseat near the window.

"Do you want me to go?" she whispered.

He bent his head.

"Do you?"

He shook his head mutely, unable to look at her.

Ann tipped his chin up with a forefinger and forced him to look her in the eye.

"I'll never leave you now, Heath. We've wasted far too much time already."

He closed his eyes, the spider web lashes sweeping his cheeks.

"I love you, princess," he said huskily. "I always have and I know I always will."

Ann leaned forward to put her arms around his neck and he gathered her to him, exhaling a long breath that caught in the middle, like a sob.

"Why don't you take me into the bedroom and prove it?" Ann whispered into his ear.

He swept her up into his arms and carried her out of the living room. Ann buried her face in his shoulder, sure that this time she would not be left alone when his passion was spent.

Heath set her on the edge of the bed and unbuttoned her blouse. "You looked so beautiful last night, you took my breath away," he said, bending to kiss the smooth shoulders he had exposed. He unhooked her bra and discarded it, undressing her carefully and gently until she was naked. Then he undressed himself, dropping his clothes on the floor and joining her on the bed.

"I'm going to make you forget everything except how much I love you," he said.

He did just that.

Later that afternoon Ann woke with Heath's arm flung across her, his head pillowed on her breast. Her previous awakenings had always been marred by finding him crowded over to his side of the bed— careful, even in his sleep, not to touch her. Now she ran her fingers through his hair and dragged her nails lightly across the nape of his neck. He stirred and his lashes lifted.

"Hi," she said.

He smiled, and she was perfectly happy.

"Do you know what tonight is?" he asked, stretching and yawning elaborately.

"The first night of the rest of our lives?" she asked, and he laughed.

"Well, that, too," he said. "But it's also Christmas Eve."

"Aha! That's why that gigantic tree is standing in the front hall. I was wondering about that."

"Let's go Christmas shopping."

"I've already been shopping, Heath."

"Well, I haven't. The personnel office takes care of corporate gifts, but I want to get something for you, and the Jensens, and Daniela and Victor and lots of other people. I'm in a benevolent mood."

"Do you know what the stores will be like tonight, Heath? Are you planning on bringing your Uzi?"

"Come on, where's your Christmas spirit? Fighting your way through the throng is half the fun."

"I've already fought my way through several throngs. Pritchard's last week looked like the Roman triumph crowd scene from *Ben Hur*. I half expected to run into Charlton Heston and his chariot in the luggage department."

Heath chuckled. "But you'll brave it all again for me, won't you, darling?" he said.

She sighed. "Do I have a choice?"

"No. And I am going to make a reservation at Lusardi's for a late dinner this evening to celebrate our—" he stopped.

"What?"

"Rapprochement," he said, and she smiled.

"Say what?" she asked.

"Don't laugh at me," he said, throwing off the sheet and going into his closet, emerging with his robe belted around his waist. "I am determined to put some flesh on those bones. You are going to have a stuffed artichoke heart, a Mediterranean salad, three-cheese lasagna, and *tiara misu* for dessert."

"I am not going to have anything, Heath—you'll never get a table for Christmas Eve at this late hour."

"I'll get one," he said firmly. "I'm going to see if Daniela left us any coffee. Be right back. Don't go away."

Ann fell back against the pillows contentedly, drawing the sheet up to her neck. She was remembering his caresses with satisfaction when the phone at her elbow rang shrilly.

Ann lifted the receiver on the night table and said, "Hello?"

"So you survived the party," Amy said.

"Barely. I'm afraid to leave the house, I might trip over a dead body in the driveway."

"How's Heath?" Amy asked cautiously.

"Heath is just the most wonderful man in the world," Ann replied, a smile in her voice.

"What happened?" Amy asked sharply.

"Rapprochement," Ann answered.

"What the hell is that?"

"Kind of like detente, except between people instead of countries," Ann said.

"Holy smokes."

"Yup."

"You have to give me all the details."

"Not now," Ann said. "Heath is home."

"He came home early for Christmas Eve?"

"He didn't go to the office today. There's a reform movement under way."

"Oh, I see."

"I am now considering having about six of his children. Maybe seven."

"That must have been quite a post-party turnaround."

"It was."

Amy chuckled wickedly. "Leave it to Heath. When he turns on the charm, he takes no prisoners."

"I believe he really wants to make it work, Amy," Ann said seriously.

"I'm sure he does. I've never doubted that he loves you, Annie. He's just always been . . . difficult."

"We talked about the past and got things straightened out, but I'll tell you all about it later. Right now I have to get dressed. Heath wants to go Christmas shopping."

"Tonight? That's a death wish. Good luck. Wear your flak jacket."

"By the way, why did you take off last night?" Ann asked. "I didn't know you were staying at the inn until after you were gone. I wanted you to spend the night here."

"I figured you and Heath were better off left alone, and wasn't I right?"

Ann laughed. "What are you doing for Christmas?"

"Going to my mother's. Have you heard from Tim?"

"Yes, he's spending the holiday with his college roommate in Massachusetts."

"Thanks to you. Otherwise he'd be spending it in a less congenial place."

"Thanks to Heath, you mean."

"Well, I'll let you go. Merry Christmas. From what you've told me, I'm sure yours will be very merry. I'll be at my mother's until Thursday. Give me a call later on in the week."

"Okay. Bye-bye."

Ann hung up the phone and got out of bed, walking naked to the bathroom and turning on the shower. She was standing under the rushing water, soaping herself with fragrant lather, when the frosted-glass shower door slid back and Heath stepped in behind her.

Ann gasped as his hands enclosed her breasts and he pulled her back against him. She closed her eyes as his strong fingers moved over her, slick with soap, slipping smoothly over her buttocks and between her legs, caressing her until she turned restlessly in his arms and pressed herself against him.

"What do you want?" Heath asked. She reached for him, twining her legs with his as the water gushed over them.

"You know," she moaned.

"Say it," he said.

"Take me," she whispered, wrapping her arms around his neck, both of them slick as seals and dripping with suds.

He lifted her and turned abruptly, pinning Ann against the wall and entering her in the same movement. It was quick and explosive, leaving them both drained and leaning against each other, laughing weakly.

"Heath, what are we doing?" Ann said, reaching for the taps and turning off the water. "This is dangerous, we could have slipped and been killed in here."

"What a way to go," Heath replied, stepping out of the stall and tossing her a towel.

"I think we should stick to the bed in future," Ann said, wiping her face.

Heath sighed. "You're so conventional."

The telephone rang in the bedroom and Heath went to answer it before Daniela could get it in the kitchen. When Ann came in after him she saw from the expression on his face as he hung up the phone that it was not good news.

"What is it, Heath?" she asked. "What's the matter?"

Heath looked at her directly. "There's a bench warrant out for your brother's arrest. The D.A. says he violated the terms of his bail by traveling to Massachusetts."

Chapter 9

Ann looked stricken. "What do you mean? You said that Tim had been given permission to go!"

"Calm down, I'm going to handle it," Heath said firmly. "Obviously some wires have crossed somewhere. Harry Caldwell is going to straighten this out, pronto."

"He won't be in his office now, Heath!"

"I'll find him wherever he is. For what I'm paying him, he'll solve this little problem if he has to take a dogsled from Springfield to Boston." Heath went to his closet and started to dress, pulling trousers off a hanger.

"I'm going with you," Ann said, dropping her towel and walking past him.

"You are not. You almost passed out last night, and after this day, you've had enough stress for at least a week. I'll go over to Caldwell's office and you stay here and relax."

"Heath, I can't ask you to keep unscrambling my messes like this," Ann protested.

"Why not? Wasn't that our deal?"

"I thought our deal was off."

"Not that part of it. Listen, you're my wife. I have the capability of handling this, and you don't." He grinned. "When I need a grammatically phrased letter, I'll let you take over. Now, get out of my way and go and pick out an outfit for later. This will all be settled in two hours, I promise you." He picked up his jacket and slung it over his shoulder, then kissed her on the cheek.

Ann stared after him as he left the bedroom, and she heard him speaking to Daniela in the hall. Then she dressed quickly and went out to the kitchen herself.

Daniela was washing dishes in the sink. The debris of the party was still visible, but reduced; Daniela had been busy clearing it away all day.

"Still at it, Daniela?" Ann said, walking over to the terrace doors and glancing outside. The furniture was stacked to one side and Victor was standing on a garden chair, taking down a string of colored lights.

"There's a lot to do," Daniela said, glancing at her and smiling. "You look so relaxed this evening."

Ann smiled back at her. It was true. Despite Tim's latest crisis, Heath's changed attitude was like a balm to her soul, giving her hope for the future and their life together.

"I guess it must be a relief to have the party out of the way," Daniela said.

Ann nodded.

"Do you want something to eat?" Daniela asked.

Ann shook her head. " No, thanks. I'm having a late dinner with Heath."

"You're too skinny, Señora Bodine. Have a snack now. Mr. Bodine, he is always telling me to cook for you, fatten you up."

"Always?" Ann said.

"Yes, since you got married."

So while Heath was giving Ann a hard time to her face, he was sneaking around behind her back and telling the housekeeper to prepare special meals for her. Typical.

"Okay, I'll have some toast," Ann said, sitting down in the breakfast nook.

Daniela went to get the bread, saying, "The party was a big success, *señora?*"

"Yes, thank you," Ann replied, thinking about its lurid aftermath with Ben Rowell in the bedroom. "You and Victor were such a big help, Heath and I appreciate it. When are you leaving?"

"We were through at noon," Daniela replied, "but I didn't want this mess to greet me day after tomorrow, so we've stayed to get some of it out of the way."

"You don't have to stay any longer."

"But, *señora,* the tables from the caterers have to go back, and the rest of the decorations—"

"Can all wait until after Christmas. Heath said that your daughter is coming to visit tonight and that should take precedence. Did Heath give you your bonus?"

Daniela nodded as she buttered toast and then put the plate in front of Ann.

"Then get lost," Ann said, laughing.

Daniela was obviously pleased. "I hope the new year is a very happy one for you, *señora,*" she said, patting Ann's arm and then walking out of the room.

That gave Ann pause. So Daniela and her husband had not been insensitive to the undercurrents of tension in the house. And Ann had tried so hard to pretend that everything was fine.

After Daniela and Victor left, a holiday hush settled over the evening, leaving Ann with nothing to do. She was too jittery to work and everybody she knew to call or visit was sure to be busy. Finally, she could wait no longer and dialed Harold Caldwell's office. She got a voice message saying that the office was closed.

If Heath and the lawyer were there, they weren't answering the phone.

Ann tried to read and to watch television, and she was just about to call again when Heath came through the door, carrying several wrapped packages and wearing a red felt Santa Claus hat with white faux fur trim.

"Ho, ho, ho," he said, encircling her with his free arm. "Oh, dear, my Mrs. Claus looks somewhat worried. Where's my joyous Christmas face?"

"How is Tim? What's happening? Is he in jail?"

"Take it easy, he's not in jail," Heath replied, dumping his packages on the entry-hall table. "Harold Caldwell pulled some rabbits out of a hat and the bench warrant has now been rescinded. Curfew will not ring tonight."

Ann sighed and closed her eyes. "I tried to call Caldwell's office," she said.

Heath grinned. "I kept him busy—he wasn't taking any outside calls."

Ann flung her arms around his neck. "Thank you. I seem to be saying that a lot lately."

"*De nada.* Hey, you haven't commented on my holiday accessory." He swept off the hat and bowed.

"Very fetching. Where did you get it?"

"I bought it at the liquor store."

"Liquor store? Have the proprietors branched out into haberdashery?"

"Nah, they had a counter display of them when I went in there to send a bottle to Ben Rowell. I couldn't resist."

"I hope you got him something nice."

"A fifth of Glenlivet."

"Good." Ann kissed him tenderly on the cheek.

"Don't you want to open your presents?" he asked, picking up the smallest one and shaking it suggestively.

"Isn't that supposed to wait until tomorrow?"

"There are no rules for a Bodine Christmas. Come on, just this one package. I want to see what you think of it."

"I thought we were going to go shopping together," Ann said, accepting it.

"We will, we will. Everything is open late tonight. Tear into that one now."

Ann went into the living room and sat on the sofa, ripping off the gold paper and red bow. Inside was a jeweler's box.

"Heath, what did you do?" Ann asked, lifting the lid.

"I made a start on the rest of our lives, I hope," he replied, watching her face.

Against a bed of deep blue velvet lay a gold chain with a large charm attached. Ann lifted it to look at it more closely; it was an old-fashioned quill and inkstand made of heavy gold and studded with diamonds.

"Heath, its beautiful. But why the charm?"

"Because you're a writer. And a pretty good one, too, I might add."

She looked at him. "How do you know?"

"I've been reading your next book."

Ann stared at him, stunned. "What? How?"

"At night, after you're asleep, I've been going into the den and breaking into your computer."

"How did you get into the file?"

He winked. "I'm a mechanical whiz, remember?"

She couldn't get over it. "Heath, you are incorrigible."

"Yes, I know. I also know more about the Italian Renaissance than I ever thought was possible."

Ann laughed.

"How long were you in Italy?"

"Not long enough. I still have more research to do."

"We'll go together." He held out his arms. "Don't I get another kiss?" he asked.

Ann flew into his arms and he pressed her close, rocking her back and forth gently.

"I'm going to make it all up to you," he said softly. "I know I've been a first-class jerk, but if I'm a very good boy, do you think you can forgive me?"

Ann held him tightly, too emotional to respond.

"I never wanted anyone but you," he said. "I tried to tell myself otherwise, tried to have relationships with other women, but it never worked. The memory of you was always there in the background, and it's like a miracle to have you here with me now. We can make a go of it, can't we?"

Ann nodded against his shoulder.

He held her at arm's length to look at her. "Annie, are you crying again?"

"I'm afraid so."

"Don't you know that we're supposed to be having a wonderful time?"

"I am having a wonderful time." She wiped her eyes with the back of her hand.

"I'm glad to hear it. Now, are we going to hit those stores or not?"

"We are."

"Let's go."

He took her by the hand and led her toward the door.

By the time they reached Lusardi's, the parking lot was packed despite the late hour and the weather, which had turned colder. Ann hugged her coat close about her as they walked inside, where Heath was greeted like a long-lost relative.

"Did you ever eat or sleep at home before we were married?" Ann asked dryly. They were being led to a secluded table near the Victorian Christmas tree that dominated the dining room.

"Not often," he admitted. "As you so astutely pointed out, nobody was there."

The maître d' seated them and had a little chat with Heath before handing them the menus. The London Philharmonic's Christmas album played softly in the background and a gas log blazed in a fireplace in a corner behind them.

"It almost feels like a Christmas up north tonight, the temperature has dropped so much," Ann said.

"That's all right, it puts me in the mood," Heath said. "I always associate Christmas with New England, anyway."

Ann laughed. "What are you talking about? You've spent every Christmas in Florida with the palm trees."

"Not when I was in the navy."

"Oh, that's right, I forgot. Where were you?"

"Mystic, Connecticut, for two years."

Ann was silent.

"What?" he said, looking at her.

"There's so much about your life since I left Florida that I don't know," she said quietly.

"What do you want to know?"

"Were you happy?"

"No," he said.

"What? Making millions of dollars?"

"I was successful. I wasn't happy."

"Some might say there's no difference."

"There is. You can take my word for it, I'm an expert. Taking revenge on people is not the path to fulfillment."

The wine steward appeared at Heath's elbow and asked if they would like a drink.

Heath looked at Ann, then shook his head.

"Nothing for either one of us," he said.

"Sworn off the stuff?" Ann asked, smiling.

"I don't seem to need it anymore." He covered her hand with his bigger one.

"Who else did you want to take revenge on, besides me?" Ann asked.

"You know. You said it once. All the golfers in the pastel polo shirts, everybody who looked through me as if I were invisible when I was a kid."

"What did you do?"

"Oh, I made sure they knew that I was in their league now, and used my money effectively to get the point across. I hired people like Joe to run my company to rub their blue noses in my prosperity. But of course I really wasn't accepted by them, no matter what I did."

Ann said nothing.

"Money doesn't make those people respect you. It's background and breeding that count. You're one of them, Princess, and you always will be, even if you don't have a dime."

"They must respect your accomplishments."

"My invention, you mean? A lucky accident. They have to deal with me now because of my business, but you'll notice I'm not getting invited to their homes."

"Neither am I, now," Ann informed him.

Heath shook his head. "You're undergoing a temporary disgrace because of your brother. That's different. You're inside the fence, and I'm outside it."

"But I'm married to you!"

"So you married down."

"Oh, Heath, you dwell too much on all of that."

"You would, too, if you'd had my early life."

"When we first got back together, I thought that's why you wanted to marry me, to show everybody on Lime Island that you could snag Henry Talbot's daughter."

Heath looked at her across the table and said, "That may have been part of it when we first met as kids. You represented the world I never had access to, the better life that was always closed to me. But once I got to know you, you were so sweet and unlike what I had expected...."

"What did you expect?"

"A snob," he said.

"I guess I did nothing to correct that impression initially, bitching at you when your repair job disturbed my nap."

He laughed. "But you were so cute standing there, hands on hips, all angry and barefoot in your bikini. I was lost from the moment I saw you."

Ann grinned. "You certainly didn't act like it."

"Oh, well, I was always very careful to cover myself in those days."

"You still are, Heath. That's what the past month has been about, right?"

He nodded thoughtfully. "I guess you've got my number, Princess."

"Just remember that," Ann said archly.

"Are you ready to order now, Mr. Bodine?" their waiter said to Heath.

They looked at each other. They hadn't even glanced at the menus on the table.

"You come here a lot, Heath," Ann said. "Just get whatever you want for both of us."

Heath ordered for them and then lifted a muffin from the basket on the table. "Have one of these, they're good. You are hereby ordered to gain ten pounds in the next two months."

Ann groaned.

"Come on, baby. You know I'm right. You don't eat enough, you never did."

"It's Christmas, Heath. Do we have to have the nutrition lecture now?"

"You're going to my doctor as soon as the holidays are over," he said firmly.

"Why?"

"For a checkup."

"There's nothing to check. I'm just thin."

"Too thin."

"That's a matter of opinion. Anyway, I'll gain weight when I'm pregnant."

His hand froze in the act of popping loose muffin crumbs into his mouth.

"What's the matter?" Ann said at the look on his face. "We haven't been doing anything to prevent it."

He said nothing.

"Don't you want to have children?" she said, alarmed at his reaction.

"I didn't think it would come up just yet," he said carefully. "I assumed we'd have some time to ourselves for a while. After all, we've been apart so long."

"Of course, but can't you imagine a little boy who looks just like you, with huge dark eyes and that glorious thick black hair?" Ann said dreamily.

"And my father's glorious heritage of alcoholism?" Heath said flatly.

"Nobody's family is perfect, Heath. Look at mine."

"Your father wasn't a stumbling drunk."

"He was an unfeeling autocrat. Is that so much better?"

"In my eyes, yes. Your old man wasn't an ongoing embarrassment."

"He was a dictator who almost ruined my life! Look what happened to us because of his interference."

Heath sighed heavily and leaned across the table to touch her cheek. "Princess, let's not argue about this now, not tonight of all nights. Look, here's our salad. I'm going to watch and make sure you eat all of it."

"Yes, sir." Ann let the subject drop but resolved to bring it up again another time. They finished the leisurely meal, talking about other things, and by the time they drove home Ann was full, tired and ready for bed.

Heath locked the front door behind them and said, "This is the first Christmas I haven't been alone in a long time."

"I find that hard to believe."

"Well, I was usually at parties, which on holidays is often worse than being alone." He put his hand on the small of her back and pushed her along toward the bedroom.

"I ate too much," Ann said as they crossed the threshold. "I can hardly walk."

"You ate like a normal human being, and if you can do it once, you can do it again. I'll make sure you do." He stood behind her and unzipped her dress, letting it slip to the floor. He lifted her hair off her neck and kissed her nape lingeringly, then unhooked her bra and dropped that on top of the dress. Ann turned in his arms and he picked her up, carrying her toward the bed.

Ann fell back on the pillows, her arms above her head. He dropped onto the bed with her, covering her slight body with his muscular one as he pulled off her briefs.

Ann wound herself around him, sighing. "I dreamed of this so many times, spent years wondering what it would be like, thinking about what I had lost forever. And now I've found it again."

Heath stood to remove his clothes, and Ann watched as the body she had desired since her adolesence was revealed, sculpted like an artist's clay figure, totally male. She reached out eagerly and he rejoined her, pulling her to him and running his hands down the satiny curve of her spine. Her fingers sank into his shoulder blades as he turned and set her back on the bed, kissing her everywhere he could reach as her eyes closed luxuriously. Then he positioned her body, encircling her waist with his arm and easing her under him.

"I love you," he said as he entered her.

"I love you, too," Ann whispered.

And that was all they needed to say.

On Christmas night, Heath and Ann were sitting in the living room, relaxing in front of a fire that was more ceremonial than necessary, when the doorbell rang. Heath, who was wearing the cashmere sweater Ann gave him for Christmas, looked at Ann inquiringly.

"Are you expecting anybody?" Ann asked.

Heath shrugged.

Ann slipped out of Heath's embrace, put down her glass of eggnog and went to answer the door. Her brother Tim was standing on the other side of it, a large wrapped box under one arm.

"Timmy!" Ann shrieked, and threw her arms around him, causing him to rock back and drop the overnight bag he was carrying in his free hand.

"Merry Christmas," Tim said, and hugged her back.

Heath hovered in the background, all smiles.

"What are you doing here?" Ann asked, releasing him and leading him into the house. "I thought you were going to stay up in Massachusetts."

"Heath got me a seat on a plane today. After my latest trouble, he thought it would be best for me to come here and let you see for yourself that I was all right." Tim stepped around his sister and reached his hand out to Heath, who shook it.

"Thanks, man," Tim said.

"*De nada,*" Heath replied.

"No. I mean, really, thanks for everything. I know that I've said it a hundred times on the phone, but you certainly deserve to hear it once again."

Ann stood looking from one man to the other, her eyes huge and sparkling.

"Come on, Tim, it's a holiday. Let's go inside and talk about something positive before your sister gets all weepy. Do you want a drink?" Heath said.

Tim shook his head ruefully. "Nah, booze tends to make me think I can win at the crap tables again."

"Well, there are no crap tables here. How about some eggnog? Nothing in it but lots of calories. We've been trying to fatten your sister up."

"That sounds like a good idea. Eggnog is fine."

They went back to the living room and indulged in meaningless chitchat for about fifteen minutes before Heath rose and said, "Well, I've still got a few presents to wrap and I'm sure you two would like to be alone for a while."

Ann shot him a grateful glance and then turned back to her brother, who was watching her closely.

"He doesn't have any presents to wrap, does he?" Tim said knowingly.

"I don't think so."

"Neither do I. You look very happy," he said.

"I am."

"That's some great guy you've got there."

"I know."

"I was so humiliated about all of this that I didn't even want to talk to him on the phone the first time, but he never acted judgmental about my problems, he just addressed what had to be done. Is he always like that?"

"Not always," Ann said dryly.

Tim scratched the back of his neck, looking so much like their father for a moment that her heart skipped a beat. Tim had Henry Talbot's patrician features and rangy build, and just about all of his gestures, too.

"Heath must really be crazy about you," Tim said.

Ann smiled.

"I mean, I know he didn't jump into this feet-first and head up the rescue team just for *me*."

Ann nodded.

"Ironic, isn't it? Heath is bailing out the company, and the son, of the man who detested him. Somewhere in the wings, the fates are laughing."

"None of it seems very funny to me," Ann replied, sighing. "How are you doing, anyway?"

Tim smiled ruefully. "One day at a time, as they say. I was doing pretty well, actually, until that bench warrant business. The thought of going back to jail really had me spooked."

"I'm sorry about that, Tim. There was some legal mixup, it never should have happened—"

Tim held up his hand to stop her. "Don't apologize to me, Annie. Everything bad that has hap-

pened in my life is my fault. That's one of the things
you learn in recovery—to take responsibility for your
own actions. Sure, our dear daddy was a bastard and
he let me know every minute of my life that I was a
bitter disappointment to him, but he's dead now, I'm
alive, and I've got to clean up *my* mess. With the help
of your husband, of course. And you."

Ann leaned forward to pour him a glass of eggnog
from the cut glass decanter on the table. "Timmy,
why did you do it?" Ann said, handing her brother
the drink. "I've never asked you, but I've always
wondered."

"The gambling?"

"Yes."

He sighed. "Well, I guess you've got a right to
know if anyone does. The answer is, I don't fully understand it myself, not yet, anyway. It has something
to do with the power I felt when I won, the power
over my life that was so lacking when Dad was alive.
I got hooked on that when I was just a kid."

Ann nodded.

"The problem is you don't always win, but you
keep going back to get that kick, convinced that
sooner or later it will happen again," Tim went on.
"And in the meantime, you're losing. And I lost big.
But part of the illness is, you're always convinced that
you *will* make that big score that will wipe out the
loans and the debts and let you start over with a clean
slate. And there's plenty of scumbags around to feed
that illusion while they're plying you with perks and
taking your money. It sucks you in, believe me."

"You should have talked to me about it, Tim. You
should have talked to *somebody*."

He closed his eyes. "I know that now." He opened them. "But when you're in that whirlpool you really think you can handle it, that the next big win will be your last."

"Why?"

"Because it's an addiction, Annie. Why does a heroin addict keep sticking needles in his arms when his veins are collapsing and his skin is a mass of scabs and his last meal was a can of orange soda? Why does an alcoholic keep drinking when he's bloated from liver failure and yellow with jaundice and can't remember what he's done for hours and days at time? It isn't logical behavior, it's an illness."

Ann put her hand over his. "I'm sorry I asked you about it," she said quietly. "Anyway, that isn't the point now, the point is to get you well."

He bit his lip, not looking at her. "I'll pay you back for what you've done for me, both of you. If I have to work at it for the rest of my life, I promise I'll pay you back."

Ann squeezed his fingers. "Why don't we just change the subject, okay? It's Christmas, let's have some Christmas cheer. Heath and I were just going to have a light supper. You'll join us, okay?"

He looked up. "Okay."

"And stay the night?"

He nodded.

"When can I unwrap that huge box and see what you brought me?" Ann asked.

He laughed. "After dinner."

Ann got up to go into the kitchen and said, "Come on with me. You can help."

Her brother followed her out of the room.

Chapter 10

"So Tim won't have to go to trial at all?" Ann asked, watching Heath's face.

"No. He's pleading guilty to a lesser charge of embezzlement and mishandling of company funds."

"What will he get for that?"

"Probably a suspended sentence in exchange for continuing with his twelve-step program and community service. And he'll have to pay the money back, of course, but I'll do that initially and then we can work out a payment schedule for him to reimburse me."

Ann flung herself on Heath, knocking him off-balance and sending him into the bedroom wall.

"Hey, hey, take it easy," he said, laughing and catching her in his arms. "It isn't over quite yet, these legal procedures always go on forever, you know that. But things are definitely looking up for your brother."

"I don't know how to thank you."

"I'm sure we can think of something," he replied, bending her backward and kissing her neck. "Now, what time is your appointment with Dr. Langley?"

"Heath, I am going, don't worry about it."

"You've been saying that for two months. We discussed this at Christmas and it's now February. You're half finished with your book, you've done an outline projecting it into a series, and you've redecorated the den. You've found time for all of these things but not for the ten-minute drive to Langley's office. I'm beginning to wonder what's going on here."

"My appointment is for eleven, and after that I'm having lunch with Amy at La Crêpe. Okay?"

"Okay, Princess," he said, and released her reluctantly. "I'm going to be at the Big Palm office all day. You can reach me there if you need me."

"I always need you," she said.

He smiled as he picked up his jacket and slipped into it. "The feeling is mutual," he said.

"Are you sure you don't have time for breakfast?" Ann asked, brushing her hair.

"Nah, I'm late already. But make sure you eat— I'm going to check with Daniela when I come home. And remember, we're having dinner with the Jensens tonight."

"I remember."

He kissed her cheek and went out into the hall, and Ann resumed her toilette.

Dr. Langley proved to be a cheerful general practitioner with wire-rimmed glasses and an intense curiosity about the woman who had married Heath Bodine.

"So how did you two meet?" Langely asked as he took Ann's blood pressure.

"Actually, we knew each other years ago, when we were kids on Lime Island," Ann said.

"Kind of lost touch, huh?" Langley said, making a notation in her file.

You could say that, Ann thought dryly as she nodded.

"I never thought Heath would get married," Langley said. "Since I've known him, five years I guess, he's lived for his business, didn't seem to have much time for emotional involvements."

"I guess the time comes sooner or later for everybody," Ann said lightly.

"So you knew him before he made his money," Langley said, feeling the glands at the sides of her throat.

"Yes."

"What was he like then?"

"Intense, quiet, very good with machinery."

"Doesn't sound like he's changed much," Langely said, laughing as he inserted his stethoscope into his ears. He listened to her chest and back and then removed the instrument, stepping back and saying, "So, what are you doing here?"

"Heath insisted that I come. He thinks I have iron-poor blood or something."

"Have you been tired?"

"A little."

"We'll run a blood test for anemia. Any episodes of dizziness, fainting?"

"Vertigo once or twice."

"Aha. So there's more here than meets the eye."

"I haven't been passing out, doctor, just a little room spinning, unsteadiness."

"Well, you're slightly underweight and your blood pressure is low, that might account for it. Any trouble with your periods?"

Ann hesitated.

"Well?" he said, watching her.

"They've been irregular. I've only had two in the last four months and they've been scanty."

Langley bit his lip. "Any nausea, bloating?"

Ann looked at him.

He nodded. "I'll give you a referral slip to an OB/ GYN right here in the building. I can't find a thing wrong with you, but you could be pregnant."

Ann gasped. "But I've had two periods!"

He shrugged. "Some people don't stop all at once, like turning off a faucet. I could run a pregnancy test here, but you might as well get checked out by a specialist, you'll need one anyway if you *are* pregnant. Hastings is good, she's very thorough." He pulled a pad out of his jacket pocket and scribbled on a slip. He ripped off the top sheet and handed it to her.

Ann stared at it, stunned.

"Why do you seem so surprised?" Langley asked. "The possiblity hadn't occurred to you?"

"I thought as long as I was bleeding I couldn't be pregnant. It seemed logical that the excitement and tension of getting married, moving back to Florida, other personal problems, could have thrown off my cycle," Ann replied. "My brother has been in some legal trouble and it's been pretty stressful."

"Well, I could be wrong. If you don't want to wait for your appointment with Hastings, take a home pregnancy test. They're quite accurate."

Ann nodded. "How do you think Heath will react to the news, if you are pregnant?" Langley asked.

"I hope he'll be happy," Ann said softly.

"Of course he'll be happy. With a beauty like you, he will make gorgeous babies."

"Doctor, just in case you talk to him, don't say anything about this until I tell him, okay? I want it to be a surprise."

"Sure, sure, I understand. But get in to see Hastings as soon as possible, okay? Your symptoms could mean other things—adhesions, endometriosis. You should be checked. Don't you have a regular gynecologist?"

"In New York."

"Go back to that doctor then if you feel more comfortable. But you'll need somebody local if you plan to have the baby here, to oversee the pregnancy. Just don't neglect this, okay?"

"All right."

Ann left the doctor's office with mixed feelings of elation and nervousness. She was certainly thrilled, but she couldn't forget Heath's reaction when she'd brought up the subject of having children on Christmas Eve.

Would he feel differently now if he knew the possibility had become reality? As she drove to the restaurant to meet Amy, she kept mulling it over in her mind, considering alternatives, trying to decide what to do.

On the way there she bought a home pregnancy test at the Lime Pharmacy.

She would make sure of what was happening before she said anything to Heath.

Amy was waiting outside the restaurant when Ann pulled up in her car. Amy waved enthusiastically as Ann approached, then hugged her friend as they walked into the restaurant.

"I'm so glad you could make it," Ann said to Amy. "You're just down for the weekend?"

Amy nodded. "I'm flying back to New York late tomorrow afternoon."

"How's your mother?"

"The same. Buying new furniture for the living room. The floor was covered with swatches." She surveyed Ann slyly. "So, how is life in the revamped Bodine marriage?" she asked as they waited for the hostess to seat them.

"Wonderful," Ann replied.

"Yes, I could tell that by the new wheels you're driving. Do you know how much that car costs?"

Ann looked at her. "Haven't a clue. Heath leased it for me last month. I couldn't drive his RV or his motorcycle, and living in New York I didn't need a car."

"Didn't you go with him to get it?"

"No, he just drove it home one day."

Amy shook her head as the hostess led the two women to a table. "You're a rare specimen, Annie. I've always known it."

"I'm not interested in cars, Amy, you know that," Ann said as she sat.

"Or anything else but Heath and those books you write," Amy replied, sitting across from her.

"You're wrong, Amy," Ann replied as she took her menu from the hostess.

Amy raised her brows inquiringly as the hostess walked away from them.

"I'm interested in knowing whether or not I'm pregnant," Ann said, and Amy let out a whoop.

Several of their fellow diners seated nearby turned to look at them.

"Please control yourself," Ann said.

"Are you sure?"

"No. I'm going to take a home test, but the doctor I saw this morning thinks I may be."

"Oh, dear, I'm so jealous," Amy said mournfully. "Here I am, still dating twenty different varieties of Mr. Wrong, and you're married with a baby on the way."

"It's still not certain."

"Oh, of course it is, doctors know. What do you think Heath will say?"

"That's my biggest concern at the moment."

They paused in their conversation as the waitress arrived and they gave their orders. When the woman walked away, Amy leaned across the table and said, "What do you mean, your biggest concern? Doesn't he want children?"

"He acted very weird when we discussed it."

"When was that?"

"Christmas."

"Well, he had just learned that you'd been telling him the truth about leaving him. Maybe he was just overwhelmed."

"I don't think so," Ann said worriedly.

"Why?"

"Well, he went into this big speech about his father being an alcoholic and not wanting to pass that problem on to the next generation."

"Oh."

"I told him every family has problems, but I don't think I was getting through to him."

"Well, you know how abysmal his childhood was. It's understandable that he would have some negative feelings on the subject."

"But some people in his situation resolve to make it better for their children. They want to take special care to be loving and attentive and interested and understanding. They want to be the opposite of the parents who hurt them. It's really the only way to deal constructively with a history like that."

"Are you talking about yourself now?" Amy asked quietly, fiddling with her napkin.

"Maybe. I know I'll never treat a child of mine the way my father treated me."

"Heath doesn't have your temperament," Amy said. "He's bound to react differently."

Ann shrugged.

"He must know you haven't been using birth control," Amy said dryly. "What does he think is going to happen?"

"He doesn't seem concerned about it. I've told him my periods have been irregular, that's one of the reasons he insisted on the doctor's visit. Maybe he thinks I can't conceive."

"Annie, I cannot believe that you haven't discussed this with him."

Ann sighed. "I've tried, but he's a magician at changing the subject, and I haven't wanted to argue with him. Things have been so lovely since the holidays, I hate to burst the bubble."

"And you think this bulletin just may do that?" Amy inquired, concerned.

"I don't know."

The waitress returned with two glasses of iced tea and set them on the table. "Lunch will be right up," she said, and walked away.

"Remember how your mother used to laugh at us, drinking iced tea all year long?" Amy said.

Ann nodded, smiling.

"It will be all right, Annie," Amy said softly.

Ann looked away from her. "If I am pregnant, of course I want the baby. But if I lost Heath now, I think I would die," she said.

"You won't lose him. He's crazy about you."

"He's crazy about me as long as I do what he wants," Ann replied flatly.

"Oh, come on. You're making him sound very cold."

"A side of him is. You're forgetting the person who made that lovely marriage-blackmail proposal a few months ago. He's still in there, along with the charmer who selects exquisite jewelry and leases expensive cars."

"And bails brothers out of jail."

"Right."

"Nobody ever said Heath wasn't complex."

"Certainly not me."

Amy raised her glass of iced tea. "Drink up. Odds are all will be well. Now, let me tell you about my latest dating fiasco, the supposedly available publishing executive who turned out to have a darling little wife and four fetching kiddies tucked away at the last stop on the commuter line.''

Ann laughed and tried to listen to Amy's monologue. But her mind kept drifting back to the little box with the pregnancy test inside it, nestled in a bag in the trunk of her car.

She would use it as soon as she got home.

By the time Heath returned from work that night, Ann knew that she was pregnant. The liquid in the test tube had turned bright pink the second she completed the steps, and she had stowed the box and the plastic debris from the test in the paper bag and stuck it in the bottom of her closet. She didn't want Daniela coming across it by accident.

Heath came in whistling, his jacket slung over his shoulder, his face lighting up when he saw Ann in the bedroom.

"Don't you look pretty!" He said, admiring her turquoise silk suit. "Is that new?"

"Yes."

"Did you see Langley?"

"Yes again. He couldn't find a thing wrong with me, but he's going to run a test for anemia."

"Why?"

"I told him you thought I had iron-poor blood."

Heath laughed. "He'll be accusing me of practicing medicine without a license."

"I must say that he seemed very curious about our star-crossed union."

Heath dumped his jacket on a chair. "He thinks I'm an anomaly, and I guess I am, in a way. He doesn't know too many self-made millionaires."

"Who does?"

"I'll bet he was impressed with you," Heath said, changing to a fresh shirt.

"Why?"

"You're beautiful and accomplished. He thinks I've snagged a prize."

"Just as long as *you* think that," Ann said, coming up behind him and putting her arms around his waist.

"How could I think otherwise?" he said, covering her hands briefly with his and then breaking loose to select a new jacket from his closet.

Ann put her brush and her lipstick into her handbag and slipped it over her shoulder.

"Ready?" Heath said as he emerged from the depths of his closet.

Ann nodded.

"What time are the Jensens expecting us?"

"Seven-thirty."

"Then let's go."

He took her hand and they walked out to the garage.

Joan Jensen welcomed them into her modern ranch house on the leeward side of Lime Island with a broad smile.

"Here's the happy couple!" she said. "I was hoping you wouldn't be late. My appetizers are fossilizing in the oven."

Heath kissed Joan loudly on the cheek. "This woman kept me alive when we were starting Bimini," he said to Ann. "I ate here five nights a week."

"He's exaggerating," Joan said.

"Not by much."

Joe appeared, bearing drinks, and the two men retired to the den just off the hall. Ann followed Joan into the kitchen and helped her to serve up the stuffed mushrooms and pigs in blankets, making small talk and inserting toothpicks into the finger food.

"You okay, hon?" Joan said to her as she turned from the oven with a tray.

"Sure. Why do you ask?"

"Well, you've been blooming the last couple of months, and I've been relieved to see it, because right around Christmas I was really worried about you."

"Oh, my brother's legal trouble, you know. It was always on my mind."

"Of course. As I said, Joe and I were thrilled to see you so much happier lately, but tonight you seem...I don't know, preoccupied. Has there been a bad turn in Tim's case?"

"No, everything is fine. I think I've just been working too hard on my book. I went to see Heath's doctor today and he gave me a clean bill of health."

"Dr. Langley?" Joan said.

"Yes."

"I hear he's good. Joe doesn't trust anybody who hasn't been in the Keys since the Seminoles, and Langley's fairly new, so I've never seen him. We go to Dr. Rappaport on Big Palm."

"Rappaport was my father's doctor."

"Do many people connect you with Henry Talbot nowadays?" Joan asked, removing the glassine wrapper from a stack of small paper napkins.

"Not that many, you'd be surprised. People forget fast, and a lot of the old guard has changed. But, of course, with Tim's name in the news, there's some recognition."

"Does anybody give you a hard time about it?"

"A few veiled remarks, nothing major. Maybe some people would say more, but I think they're afraid of Heath."

"Afraid he'll sue them?" Joan said.

"Or punch them in the mouth. He's quite capable of either course of action."

Joan chuckled. "I remember him when he was a kid. Very tough. He hasn't changed much in that regard."

"Did you know him when he first came to work for Joe?" Ann asked.

"Sure did. All sinew, that glossy hair, huge dark eyes. He was something to see."

"I know. I saw him."

Something about the wistful note in her voice touched the older woman, and Joan patted her arm. "I'm sorry it took so long for you two to get back together," she said.

"It was a misunderstanding."

"So I gathered. But I know Heath can be pretty unforgiving. It's the opposite face of his generosity. He's a great friend but a formidable enemy."

Ann nodded.

Joan brightened. "Enough of this serious talk. Let's bring this food in to the men before they get restless," she said.

Ann picked up the napkins and a tray and went out of the kitchen with Joan.

The rest of the evening went smoothly and Ann held her tongue about her news until she and Heath were back in their bedroom. Heath decided to take a shower and Ann waited for him in their bed, dressed in a satin negligee. When he joined her, wearing only a towel about his waist and smelling of soap and shampoo, she wrapped her arms around his neck and snuggled in next to him.

"You feel nice and warm," he said. "Aren't anemics supposed to be cold all the time?"

"Heath, forget about that. I'm not anemic. I just took the test to satisfy Langley."

"What was the test?"

"A blood sample."

"When will the results be in?"

"Early next week."

"If you're not anemic, then why are you dizzy?"

"Langley thought I might be pregnant," Ann said after a long, doubtful pause.

He froze; she could feel his body stiffen against hers. "Did he examine you?"

"Not internally. He just thought that explanation might fit my symptoms."

"What symptoms?"

"The dizziness, the irregular periods."

"You said that was from stress."

"I'm not a doctor, Heath. I was just guessing. Anyway, Langley gave me a referral to an OB/GYN in his building. I called and I have an appointment next week."

Heath got out of bed and turned to face her, putting on his robe. "You can't be pregnant," he said flatly.

"I think I am, Heath. I took one of those home tests and it was positive."

His face closed completely and Ann felt a chill when she saw the old expression, hostile and withdrawn, suffuse his features. She had hoped never to see it again.

"Then the child cannot possibly be mine," he said coldly.

Chapter 11

Ann was too stunned to reply for several seconds. Then she said, "What on earth do you mean, Heath?"

"Just what I said. You're not pregnant by me."

There was an air of unreality about the exchange that made Ann wonder if she had already fallen asleep and was having a nightmare. "Are you accusing me of having an affair?"

"I don't know how else this could have happened," he said tightly, his arms folded.

"Don't be ridiculous. You know how it happened."

"No I don't. I had a vasectomy while I was in the Navy. If you're having a baby, it isn't mine."

Ann stared at him, her lips parted in disbelief. "You had a vasectomy?"

He glared back at her stonily.

"Why?" she said.

"You know why. I didn't want to produce any more congenital drunks."

"So you knew you couldn't have children when we were first married?" Ann said, dumbfounded.

"Of course. In the kind of marriage we were planning to have, it wasn't going to make any difference."

"But what about after Christmas, when things changed? Just when, exactly, were you going to share this piece of information with me?"

"Don't try to turn the tables here—the discussion at hand concerns *your* mysterious pregnancy. Who's the father?"

"You're the father, you idiot, and I'm livid that you could even imply otherwise," Ann replied, throwing back the covers on the bed and standing to face him. "You must know that vasectomies don't always work perfectly—they can still fail to prevent pregnancy in some circumstances. Instead of insulting me with this baseless accusation, why don't you contact the doctor who performed the operation and find out exactly what's going on? If you loved me, or trusted me the way you should, that would be your initial reaction, not another round of 'let's beat up on Annie.'" She marched to her closet and began to pull clothes off hangers.

"What are you doing?" he asked, following her.

"Isn't it obvious? I'm leaving." She rapidly folded an assortment of sweaters and slacks and tossed them haphazardly into a canvas flight bag.

"In the middle of the night?"

"I see no reason to stay any longer."

"You're leaving me?" he said in a bewildered tone, as if unable to believe it.

"Of course. Do you think I'm going to stay here and listen to any more of this garbage? I've been as understanding and patient as I know how to be. I forgave you for the way you treated me when we first got back together. I made every excuse I could think of for your abominable behavior and overlooked all of it in order to have the future with you that I so desperately wanted. But this is the last straw, Heath. If you actually think that I have been sleeping with somebody else during the past couple of months when we've been so happy together, then I don't even know what to say to you."

"It may have happened before Christmas," he said flatly, his gaze level.

"Oh, I see. While you were torturing me on a daily basis, I was taking comfort in some other man's arms?"

"Why not? According to you, I gave you sufficient reason. How pregnant are you?"

"I don't know. I'd have to have a sonogram to date the conception. But no matter when this baby was conceived, it is yours, and I will undergo DNA testing to prove it. I'll send you the results in the mail." She tore off her nightgown furiously and then pulled a sweater over her head.

"Where are you going?"

"To my apartment in New York. We've continued to pay the rent on it, if you recall, and it's empty. You suggested it as a refuge once before. It's as good a place as any for me to be."

"Wait . . ." he said, grabbing her arm.

Ann tore it loose from his grasp, and when his eyes met hers again he saw that, despite her reserved tone of voice, she was indeed furious.

"No, I won't wait. I love you, Heath. I have always loved only you—and apparently that is my misfortune. It may interest you to know that during the eleven years we were apart I never made love with another man. I was faithful to you, not only during this marriage, but all the time before when the mere memory of you made the presence of any other man pale by comparison. You have been my one and only lover, but I know that nothing I can say will convince you of that. You seem determined to drive me away, on one stupid pretext or another, and this time you have finally succeeded." Ann stepped into a pair of slacks, zipped them up and grabbed her purse with one hand and the overnight bag with the other. When he blocked her path, she stopped short.

"Get out of my way," she said through gritted teeth, her body rigid.

"Listen—"

"I have listened. I have listened to more nonsense from you than I have ever heard from another human being, including my late and unlamented father. I have had enough. Now, are you going to move, or are you planning to chain me to the bedstead and post an armed guard? Because the second you leave me alone I'll be gone."

He stepped aside and she breezed past him. She paused in the doorway and looked back at him. "You know, I was worried about telling you I was pregnant, because of your less-than-enthusiastic reception to the topic last Christmas Eve. I didn't know the reason for your negative response, of course, but it never occurred to me that you would accuse me of having another man's child. Your opinion of me must be even lower than I ever imagined. Goodbye, Heath.''

Heath stood staring after her, the finality of her last words ringing in his ears.

Ann had planned to drive to the airport and leave her car in the lot for Heath to pick up later, but she only got halfway there before a reaction set in that forced her to pull over to the side of the road. She was shaking uncontrollably, her knees vibrating like windshield wipers, and there was a tightness in her throat that refused to explode into tears. She had left Heath. Her beautiful dream was over, and it had happened in a matter of minutes.

She sat in the car, her arms propped on the steering wheel and her head bent, until a police car cruised past and slowed, its occupant regarding her curiously. Ann straightened and glided out into the traffic lane; all she needed was to be picked up by the cops now. But she suddenly felt incapable of driving the rest of the way to the airport, and then remembered that the Jensens lived only a couple of blocks away. She drove there slowly, her heart pounding, and left her car at the curb in front of the house, which was dark. They were probably asleep. She almost turned around and went back, but the thought of getting into that car again, alone, was too much.

Ann bit her lip and pressed the doorbell. Nothing happened for a long time.

She pressed it again. When there was still no response, she turned to go and was halfway down the walk when the porch light snapped on and Joan Jensen, belting a cotton bathrobe around her, yanked open the door.

"Hi, Joan," Ann said, feeling utterly ridiculous.

"Annie, is that you?" Joan said, peering nearsightedly into the darkness.

"Yes."

"What on earth are you doing here at one o'clock in the morning?" Joe asked, towering behind his wife. "Are you all right?"

"Uh, not exactly. I've left Heath."

Husband and wife stared at her with identical expressions of astonishment, which under other circumstances would certainly have been funny.

Joe recovered first, pushing his way past his wife and extending his hand to Ann.

"You poor lamb, come right inside and sit down. You look like the only survivor of a plane crash," he said, leading Ann to the plaid sofa in the living room while his wife hovered, fishing in the pocket of her robe for her glasses.

"What happened?" Joan asked.

"I can't believe this," Joe added. "You were just here tonight and everything was fine." He sat across from Ann in an armchair, his expression baffled.

"Everything was *not* fine," his wife corrected him. "I knew Ann had something on her mind."

"You're right, I did," Ann said. "I'm pregnant, and I told Heath about it when we got home. He said the baby wasn't his and accused me of having an affair."

There was a stunned silence for several seconds.

"Why, I should whip that boy within an inch of his life," Joe said first, rising from his chair.

"Settle down, Joe," his wife said warningly. "Let's hear the rest of this."

"There isn't much more to tell. He said that he'd had a vasectomy right after he got out of the navy and so he couldn't possibly be the father."

"Well, that does sort of change the picture, doesn't it?" Joe said, his brow furrowed.

"Don't be silly, Joe. If Ann is pregnant, of course Heath's the father. That he could think otherwise is disrespectful of Ann as well as their marriage," Joan said.

"I told him he should go back to the doctor who did the procedure. But regardless of what he hears, I can't live with a man who would think that of me. He didn't consider for a moment that the pregnancy might be accidental. He immediately assumed I had been unfaithful, and I'm tired of walking on egg-shells, wondering when he's going to find fault with me again."

"What you need, young lady, is a good shot of brandy," Joe said, going to get it.

"She's pregnant, Joe, remember? There's some herbal tea in the kitchen, would you put the kettle on to boil?" Joe left the room and as he did Joan turned to Ann and said, "What are you going to do?"

"I was planning to catch the next flight to New York and go back to my old apartment. But I only got this far and came here. I couldn't seem to drive any farther."

"Well, we're glad you did, honey. You certainly shouldn't be wandering around at this late hour in your present state of mind," Joan said.

Ann let her head fall wearily to the back of the sofa. "I thought Heath and I were past all of our troubles, but I guess I was wrong," she said dispiritedly.

"He should have told you about the vasectomy," Joan said. "He must have known you wanted children."

"Well, we got married under rather unusual circumstances," Ann replied.

"I thought it was kind of sudden," Joan said cautiously.

Ann sighed. "I guess I'd better tell you all of it. It might make all of this drama a little more understandable. I'm sure you must think Heath and I are both certifiable by now."

Joan waited.

"Heath blackmailed me into marrying him," Ann said. "My brother was in horrendous trouble as a result of a gambling habit, ScriptSoft was bankrupt, and everybody in the world was suing Tim. He was about to be prosecuted and stood to go to jail. Heath said he would bail Tim out of the mess if I married him."

"Why did he want that?"

"Revenge."

"Revenge?" Joan said.

"We had planned to run away together that summer we were in love, and I pulled out of the plan at the last minute, left Heath waiting for me. He thought it was because I couldn't give up the high life I enjoyed as the Talbot ingenue.''

"But that wasn't it?"

"No. My father found out about our plans and said he would have Heath arrested for statutory rape unless I left town and never saw him again."

Joan gasped. "Did you tell Heath this?"

"Yes. But he didn't believe me until the story was confirmed by a retired cop who was on the force at the time and knew that my father had investigated bringing charges against Heath."

"It sounds like your husband doesn't have much faith in you," Joan said softly.

"You're right, and that's the root cause of our problems. He just can't trust me. Maybe he can't trust any woman. His mother abandoned the family, and what happened between us when we were teenagers didn't help, even if the damage I did was unintentional. But it seems he just can't get past it."

Joan nodded somberly.

"He reads the papers, he watches the news," Ann said, gesturing vaguely. "He must know that vasectomies aren't always foolproof. I'm sure his doctor told him that at the time he had his. But he leapt to the conclusion that I had been unfaithful, because it's what some part of him wants to believe, and I'm tired of trying to overcome that presumption of guilt every day of my life. If something inside him has to spoil our happiness, then he will have to live alone."

"Why would a young, healthy man have a vasectomy?" Joan wondered aloud.

"I'm sure you've heard all the reports about alcoholism being genetic, that scientists can create alcoholic mice in the laboratory through selective breeding," Ann said. "Heath's experience with his father was so awful that he didn't want to pass the tendency on to his children."

"And at the time he had this done, you were out of his life, right? I'm sure he couldn't picture a future that would include children," Joan said.

Ann shrugged. "I don't think he was considering anything then but making money and getting ahead in the world."

"Here's your tea," Joe said, rejoining them and handing Ann a cup, which she accepted gratefully.

"Joe, did you know about this blackmail business when Heath and Ann got married?" his wife demanded of him sharply, her dark eyes narrowed.

"Sort of," Joe replied, looking sheepish.

"What does that mean?" Joan said.

"He told me about it at Christmas. I didn't know it before they got married."

"And you never said a word to me?" Joan asked, amazed at the idea.

"Heath made it clear that it was his business," Joe said, shrugging.

"I feel kind of awkward accepting your hospitality," Ann interjected, interrupting them as she took a sip of the tea. "After all, you were Heath's friends first, and here I am telling you all these terrible things about him."

"We're your friends, too," Joan said swiftly. "And you're not saying anything we didn't suspect for a long time. It was plain that Heath didn't trust women—his relationships were always brief and very surface. That's why we were elated when he married you, but we didn't realize the complicated subtext involved. All we knew was that you'd been an item as kids and were now reunited.''

"I didn't think it was appropriate to give you all the lurid details,'' Ann said dryly. "Though, of course, you wound up hearing them anyway.''

"Well, you're staying here tonight, and no excuses,'' Joan said briskly. "I'll make up the guestroom bed and in the morning, if you still want to go to New York, Joe will drive you to the airport. You can leave that article of conspicuous consumption at the curb and Heath can pick it up anytime. I don't know if I'll be able to speak to him when he does, but that's another issue.''

"Don't blame him,'' Ann said. "We're both responsible for this disaster—Heath for his inability to trust me, and me for my naiveté in thinking that we could wipe out all the damage of the past and start fresh. The past affects the present, it will always be there, like a shadow.''

"You look exhausted,'' Joan said. "Just give me a minute to get fresh sheets on the bed and we'll be in business.'' Joan left the room and Joe shifted his weight uncomfortably.

"It's really a pity about you two,'' Joe finally said quietly. "It's obvious you're crazy about each other.''

"Sometimes that isn't enough,'' Ann replied.

"It should be.''

"In a perfect world,'' Ann said dejectedly.

"Are you going to divorce him?'' Joe asked.

Ann's eyes filled with tears. "I didn't think about anything except getting out of there tonight.''

"Don't be hasty. Take some time to consider it.''

"Joe, I know how much you care for Heath, but he's a better friend than he is a husband," Ann said flatly.

"I can understand that," Joe said. "He's very... volatile. It's just that where business matters are concerned, he will usually listen to my advice."

"I only wish I could say the same about his personal life," Ann replied.

Joan returned with a blanket folded in her arms. "All set," she said.

Ann rose and followed her into the hall.

Heath paced the floor in his bathrobe, unable to leave the bedroom or to stop walking up and down restlessly. Ann was gone, and every impulse he possessed urged him to go after her. But he remained where he was, stymied not by stubbornness but by an awareness of what he had done.

He had ruined it. Over the past couple of months Ann had gradually begun to relax and believe that they could work out their problems, forget the brutal beginning to their reunion and the legacy of their former lives. But he had blasted it all into smithereens with just a few cruel words, and he had the sinking feeling that this time he would not be able to patch everything together.

He had gone too far.

Heath slid back the door to the patio and stood out on the flagstones, looking up at the stars. They began to blur and he had to glance away.

He didn't really believe that Ann had been unfaithful to him, no more than he had believed that she'd been flirting with Ben Rowell at their Christmas party. But something in him made him want to rend and tear what was good, smash it and break it and stomp it in to bits. Did he still think he wasn't good enough for Henry Talbot's daughter? Or was it that the thought of children terrified him, their neediness and total dependence, the idea that he might be as bad a father as his own father had been? He should have told Ann that, of course, instead of making stupid accusations, but admission of weakness was not in his makeup. He had pulled out of Hispaniola through toughness and determination, never letting anyone see a weak spot in his iron facade. It was too difficult to change for one new person, even if that person was Ann. His habits were fixed.

Heath sat on a redwood bench and stared at the ground, remembering the look on her face when he'd said the baby could not be his. Of course he knew that her pregnancy was possible, he had been told as much when he'd had the operation. But instead of accepting her version of events, he'd had to say the most damning thing he could think of and drive her out of the house.

Why was he so destructive?

He stood again, wondering where she had gone. She had the car and a wallet full of credit cards she rarely used, but she might find a purpose for them now. She could go anywhere in the world and he would have to hire a posse to find her.

And she was carrying his child.

The phone in the bedroom rang shrilly, startling him out of his reverie. He dashed for it, slipping on the rug, and grabbed it on the second ring.

"Annie?" he said.

"No, but she's here," Joan replied icily.

"Joan?"

"Yup."

"She's at your house?"

"Yes."

"I'll be right over," Heath said.

"I wouldn't do that," Joan said.

"Why not?"

"She's asleep now, and I think you should let her rest. She was very upset and I don't imagine waking up and seeing you is going to help her calm down, do you?"

There was a frosty tone in Joan's usually friendly voice that Heath didn't mistake.

"Then I'll talk to her in the morning," Heath said.

"I can't promise that she'll be here."

"Keep her there."

"I'll do no such thing, Heath. She's a grown woman and can do as she pleases, and what she pleases right now is to get away from you."

"Joan, she's pregnant."

"Yes, I know, and I hear the child's paternity is in doubt," Joan said sarcastically.

"Joan, this is between Ann and me."

"No, it isn't. Not anymore. Not since you drove her away and she wound up on my doorstep. I don't know why I'm even letting you know where she is—Joe said not to bother calling you—but I guess I didn't want you to worry."

"I'll be there first thing in the morning."

"Heath, I can't prevent you from doing that, but I would advise against it. I think Ann needs time."

Heath hesitated. So far he had done exactly what he wanted, and where had it gotten him? Maybe he should listen to someone else for a change.

"I'll call, then."

"All right," Joan said.

"And, Joanie? Thanks."

Joan hung up without replying.

Heath called the Jensen house at seven the next morning, after a sleepless night.

"Let me talk to Ann," He said to Joe, who answered.

"I'm sorry, Heath. She's gone. I drove her to the airport an hour ago," Joe said.

Ann's apartment was just as she'd left it. Almost. The neighbor who'd sent her things to Florida had been watering her plants, but there was a thin film of dust on all the furniture and the place had a closed-up, musty smell that made her nose twitch reflexively. She flung the windows wide, despite the frosty February temperatures, and spent the first day in therapeutic cleaning—dusting and polishing furiously to forget her troubles while a gray sleet fell outside, covering the streets of Greenwich Village with slush.

Twice she broke down crying as she was scrubbing the bathroom tile, a chore she had not missed while Daniela was doing it in Florida, but there was something satisfying about taking out her anger on soap scum and graying grout. When every surface in the four rooms was spotless and shining, she took a long shower and then made an appointment with the Fifth avenue gynecologist she'd been seeing for years.

No amount of misery was going to make her neglect the health of this baby.

When there was no more cleaning left to do, Ann sat at her computer and tried to work, but the bulk of the book was on the hard drive in Florida, and she kept forgetting references until she gave up in frustration. She would ask Daniela to send her what she needed, and maybe that would help.

For the moment, her muse had deserted her.

Disgusted and weary, Ann lay down on her bed to take a nap, telling herself that the desire for sleep was not depression but the instinct to take care of the baby.

Her phone started to ring as her head slipped to the pillow. It rang twenty times, until she lifted the receiver and let it drop back into the cradle. Then it began to ring again.

Ann unplugged it and threw the instrument into the bottom of her closet.

Then she went back to bed.

Three days later Ann was checking some references in the outdated version of the Encyclopedia Britannica she had purchased from the Dunnell Library when a furious knocking commenced at her door. She rose and stood on the rug just inside the door, saying to the dead air, "Heath, go away. I don't want to talk to you."

"It isn't Heath," Amy's voice replied in irritation. "Now will you please open this door?"

Ann undid the three dead bolts necessary for life on Astor Place and let Amy into the hallway.

"What are you doing here?" Ann said, amazed.

"Seeing if you are dead or alive, since I've been calling every day and getting no answer."

"I disconnected the phone."

"That was very smart."

"I didn't want to talk to Heath."

"Or anybody else, apparently." Amy unbuttoned her coat and removed it, shivering. "I always forget how cold it gets up here. Why do people choose to live in such an ungodly climate? I took this rag out of mothballs, and burned up the rest of my frequent flyer miles, trekking up here for the weekend when Heath told me you had left him. What the hell is going on? The last time I talked to you all was wedded bliss, and now this."

"I told him I was pregnant, and he said he wasn't the father," Ann stated flatly.

Amy's face went blank with shock. "What?" she finally said, inadequately.

"I guess he didn't tell you that part of it, did he?" Ann observed dryly.

"No." Amy followed Ann into the tiny living room and collapsed into a chair, tossing her overnight bag on the sofa. "He certainly has had you on a roller coaster, hasn't he?"

"The ride's over," Ann said.

"Does he know that?"

"I've tried to make it perfectly clear."

"Has he been here?"

Ann nodded. "I wouldn't let him in and threatened to call the police. I thought he would kick in the door until I told him if I had a miscarriage it would be his fault. I assumed he had come back when I heard you in the hall."

"Is he still in New York?"

"I doubt it. I don't think he could tear himself away from his precious business for longer than a day or two."

Amy pulled her sweater over her head and unbuttoned the top button of her shirt. "God, it's hot in here. Coming inside is like going from an ice chest into a baker's oven. No wonder everybody in New York is sick."

"Steam heat in these old buildings," Ann said, gesturing to the burbling radiator.

Amy sighed and removed her galoshes, frowning at the melting puddle of goo they had shed. "I remember that you were worried about how Heath would receive this news, but whatever gave him the idea that the child wasn't his?"

"He had a vasectomy eight years ago."

Amy stared at her. "Why would he do that?"

"So he wouldn't produce any little alcoholics like his father. At least, that's what he says."

"But you don't buy it."

"I think the whole idea of family life is so blighted for him that he just wants to avoid the issue."

"But he should have told you."

"Well, you know how we began this marriage, it didn't really come into play then. And later I think he was afraid to say anything because I let him know I wanted children."

"So rather than think medical science had failed, he assumed you had an affair?" Amy said, staring down in dismay at her equally wet shoes.

"Oh, who knows? I don't care anymore. I only know what he said and that's enough for me."

"How can you stand it here with all this sleet and snow?" Amy asked, staring out the window.

"I prefer it to the company on Lime Island," Ann replied, hanging Amy's coat in her closet.

"What have you been doing holed up in here?"

"Working. Daniela sent me my manuscript."

"How can you concentrate?"

"I couldn't at first, but it's getting better."

"Have you seen your doctor here?"

Ann nodded.

"How pregnant are you?"

"Three months, according to the sonogram."

"So it happened when you first got married."

Ann nodded.

"Heath has a lot of money. He can pursue you to the ends of the earth if he wants to."

"Let him try," Ann said grimly.

"So you're determined to fight him?"

"I'm determined to do what's best for me and the baby, whatever that may be."

"Going up against somebody who has that many resources is a formidable challenge," Amy said warningly.

"I'm equal to it," Ann replied.

Amy stared at her, then began to smile slowly.

"I believe you are," she said.

"You must be frozen, coming here directly from Florida," Ann observed. "What would you like? Something hot to eat or drink? Coffee, tea, cocoa?"

"Bourbon," Amy answered.

"I don't think I have any liquor."

"Well, look and see, will you?"

Ann went into the galley kitchen and returned with two bottles. She held them out and Amy took one look and gagged.

"That's cooking sherry," Amy said disgustedly.

"How about this other one?"

"Peach liqueur? Forget it. Why do you have to be such a teetotaler?"

"I'm not a teetotaler, I just never buy booze. I don't entertain much."

"Well, Zelda, it looks like we are going to go for a walk to that cozy little bar across the street."

"Oh, all right, if you insist." Ann was moving toward the closet when knocking sounded at her door again.

The two women looked at one another in alarm.

"Ann, it's Heath," a male voice said.

"I think I hear my mother calling me," Amy said swiftly, standing abruptly.

"Amy, if you run out on me now, I will never speak to you again," Ann whispered fiercely.

Amy looked dismayed but stayed where she was.

Ann walked over to the hall, put her mouth to the doorjamb, and said as firmly as she could, "Heath, I've already told you that I don't want to talk to you."

She could hear his heavy sigh from the other side of the paneled door.

"Ann, I've had legal advice on this," Heath replied wearily. "I can get a court order allowing me access to you if you want me to go that route."

"On what grounds?" Ann demanded.

"You sound like a lawyer," Amy whispered.

Ann held up her hand for Amy to be quiet.

"On the grounds that you're sequestered here in an emotionally disturbed state and may be endangering the life of our unborn child," Heath replied.

This remark so enraged Ann that she yanked open the door and confronted Heath, hands on hips, eyes blazing.

"How dare you?" she demanded. "Not wanting to see you means that I am emotionally *sound,* not disturbed, and since when are you concerned about the welfare of a child you don't want and furthermore claim isn't yours?"

Amy was slinking past Ann soundlessly, heading straight for the closet door.

"Stop!" Ann said, whirling to confront her.

Amy stopped.

"Why don't you let Amy go? This is embarrassing her and isn't doing much for me, either," Heath said. "We'll have to talk about this sooner or later, it might as well be now."

Ann glared at him, thinking it over as Amy looked at her hopefully.

"All right," Ann finally said.

"I'll be across the square in the Shamrock Shanty," Amy said swiftly, grabbing her coat from the closet. She gave Ann the thumbs-up sign behind Heath's head as she fled through the door and closed it behind her.

"How can you live in this place?" Heath asked, looking around him in amazement. "It's a telephone booth."

"I'm not in the mood for small talk, Heath," Ann said directly. "Get to the point."

"I want you back, you and the baby," he said.

"I take it you saw your doctor and he confirmed that you could be the baby's father?" Ann said.

"I haven't seen anyone. I know the baby is mine. You're in love with me and you wouldn't have slept with anyone else."

"And when did you receive this dramatic revelation?"

"I've known it all along."

"So you had a psychotic episode when you accused me of being unfaithful?"

Heath slumped in resignation, unable to reply. He unbuttoned the cashmere stadium coat he was wearing. "Do you think it would be possible for me to sit down? My limo didn't show up at the airport and I had to take a taxi here from Kennedy."

"What a shame," Ann said, stepping aside, no trace of sympathy in her voice.

Heath dumped the heavy coat on a chair and sat on the small sofa. He was wearing a cream-colored wool crew-neck sweater and chocolate brown slacks with his customary moccasins, which were now stained dark with dampness.

"Take your shoes off," Ann said.

He glanced up at her. "What?"

"Take your shoes off, they're soaked right through. You'll catch a cold."

He obeyed, peeling off the wet socks, too. Ann took the socks and draped them over the radiator, where they sizzled and emitted a satisfying, safe-from-the-storm odor of wet wool and steam. She shoved both of the stiffening moccasins under the radiator and turned around to face him.

"I'm not coming back," Ann said.

Heath looked at her, then away. "Ann, I'm sorry for what I said. It was uncalled for and I've regretted it ever since."

"I believe that you're sorry. This time, as you were the last time. And you'll be sorry the next time, too."

"There won't be a next time."

"There *will* be a next time, because the fundamental need to hurt me and drive me away will always be there. I can't raise a child in that atmosphere. I won't."

"So you're saying there's nothing I can do to make it right and have a life with you?"

"There is."

He eyed her suspiciously. "Like what?" he said.

"Go for counseling. I'll go with you."

His face closed. "No."

She picked up his coat and handed it to him. "Then there's nothing more to say," Ann stated.

He dropped the coat on the floor. "I'm not going to a headshrinker to dredge up all that crap from my childhood that I've been trying to forget for twenty years!"

"It's the source of your problems now, Heath. Surely you must see that."

"I don't need to be analyzed by you or anybody else, thank you very much."

"Fine. Goodbye. I think you can see the door from where you're sitting."

His eyes narrowed. "How could I have forgotten how tough you can be?"

Ann said nothing.

"I should have remembered the way you were with your father," he added.

"If I'm tough, as you put it, you've forced it on me. I'm not going to raise this child in an environment as dysfunctional as the one which surrounded you."

"And the only way to prevent that is to get rid of me?" Heath inquired.

"Or help you."

"I don't need that kind of help. We can work things out between us."

"We've tried that, Heath! How's it going?"

Heath's mouth became a hard line. "If you refuse to come back to me, I can sue you for custody once the baby is born."

"Go right ahead. I'll be very happy to say that you had an operation to prevent your ever fathering children and then denied paternity when I told you I was pregnant. I doubt very much that a judge will give custody to a man who never wanted children in the first place and would spend all his time working while the child was left in the care of servants."

He gazed at her levelly. "I see you've already thought about all of this."

"I've had plenty of time to think."

"So this is how we're going to leave it?"

"I guess so."

"What are you going to do? Stay here?"

"Yes. I have a good doctor, the hospital is two blocks away. I have plenty of work to keep me busy."

"What about the trip back to Italy?"

"It can wait until after the baby is born."

"I'll want to see it."

"I'm sure we can work out reasonable visitation rights, other people do."

"As crisp as lettuce, aren't you?" he said bitterly.

Ann relented. "Look, Heath, I know you can afford to hire a legal team that will drag me through the courts for years. For that matter, you can probably pay off anybody you want in order to make this come out exactly the way you please. But I'm asking you, for the sake of the baby, not to do that."

He was silent, then picked up his coat and put it over his arm. He stepped into his fried shoes and then draped his other arm around her shoulder and kissed her cheek.

"Don't, Heath. Please don't. That's not going to help this situation."

His arm fell. "When is the baby due?"

"The third week in August."

"I'll arrange through Caldwell to have all of your bills sent to me."

"That's not necessary."

"You're still my wife. We'll work out the details later, but I'm not going to have you scrimping along here while you're carrying this baby."

"All right."

He looked at her and she felt her heart turn over; he still had the power to turn her insides into putty. She'd better send him on his way, fast.

Ann walked to the door and opened it for him. "Goodbye, Heath," she said.

"Goodbye."

Ann waited until she heard his footsteps fade before she started to cry, staring at his smoldering socks on the radiator.

Chapter 12

"Good Lord, you're as big as a house," Joan said, laughing delightedly and patting Ann's tummy. "That baby isn't going to arrive right now, is it?"

Ann closed the door of her apartment and ushered Joan into the living room, which appeared even smaller than usual with the boxes of baby clothes and receiving blankets stacked against one wall taking up a good deal of the walking space.

"I hope not," Ann replied. "He's not supposed to be due for another two weeks."

"He?"

Ann nodded and smiled. "The ultrasound pictures say that it's a boy."

Joan walked around the reclining chair and then stopped short when she saw that it was occupied by a huge stuffed bear. The toy animal was wearing a red corduroy vest and a red-and-blue plaid satin bow.

"What in heaven's name is that?" Joan exclaimed.

"My friend Amy's contribution. She's coming for a visit soon and I've forbidden her to bring anything else. There's hardly room for the baby—I'm going to have to move out."

Joan held up several gaily wrapped gift packages and they both laughed.

"Have a seat. Would you like some iced tea? There's nothing worse than August in the city," Ann said.

"Iced tea would be lovely. It's nice and cool in here, your air conditioner must be efficient."

"It's an antique, but it works." Ann returned from the kitchenette with two tall glasses, tea for Joan and mineral water for herself.

"How long are you going to be in New York?" Ann asked, handing Joan her drink.

"Just today. My niece's wedding is this evening and I'm flying back first thing in the morning. Come on, open that one up. It's from Daniela and Victor."

Ann tore off the paper and opened the indicated box to find a hand-crocheted crib blanket, done in shades of pink and blue.

"This is gorgeous," Ann said, turning it over in admiration. "I'm so helpless with handicrafts."

"Daniela made it herself."

"How thoughtful. I'll send her a note."

"And that one's from me."

Ann opened the box to find an infant outfit trimmed in delicate lace.

"It's for a boy or a girl, three to six months."

Ann rose and kissed Joan on the cheek.

"Thank you so much," she said, blinking rapidly and looking away, fussing with the box to cover her emotion.

"Now, are we going to talk about him, or not?" Joan said, folding her hands.

"How is he?" Ann asked, sitting again and wiping her eyes with her fingers.

"Miserable. He misses you terribly."

"Has he said so?"

"You know him better than that. He says nothing, pretends that nothing is wrong. He just works twenty-four hours of every day. He and Joe are opening a new marina in Chester City. Have you heard from him at all?"

"He communicates through the lawyer."

"But isn't that what you wanted?"

"Yes. I said so, anyway. I didn't realize I would be so lonely." Ann shook her head, her eyes misting again. "I get so weepy, it must by my condition."

"I think you miss Heath."

"Of course I do."

"Then get back together with him."

"The problems will still be there."

"But, Annie, do you really want to raise this baby all by yourself?"

Ann sighed and closed her eyes. "I want to raise him with a happy, healthy father. That isn't Heath. Not now, anyway. I thought if I stayed with him and loved him he would get over the past, but I see now that it will take more than that. But I can't convince Heath. He would rather turn a blind eye and give up his family than seek the help he needs."

"I don't think he's reasoned all of that out," Joan said. "He's just in a lot of pain."

"And planning to work himself to death to forget it."

Joan shrugged.

"Is there another woman in his life?" Ann asked, wary of the question but desperate to know.

"Don't be ridiculous."

"Well, he *is* separated from me."

"Physically, maybe, but not in his mind."

Ann bit her lip. "Joan, you must have an opinion. What do you think I should do?"

"Give him another chance?"

Ann didn't answer.

"Well?"

"I can't raise a baby in constant turmoil, Joan."

"Maybe after the child comes, he'll be different."

"Why?"

"Fatherhood can have a benign effect. I've seen it happen before, believe me."

"I'd like to believe you."

"Let's shelve this depressing subject for the moment. You said on the phone last week that you sold a sequel to your book?"

"I sold the series. I'm going to do three books."

"That's exciting, isn't it?"

"I suppose so. It's a commitment on the part of the publisher, anyway."

"They must think you're very talented."

"I hope so. I just want to do the kind of work I like."

"You'll be a busy mother."

"Maybe that will help."

"Help what?"

"To fill the void."

"Annie, why don't you call him? I'm sure he's just waiting for the phone to ring."

Ann shook her head. "I'm not being stubborn, Joan. I know what will happen. We'll get together, things will be wonderful for a while, and then something will come up to trigger that rage he's got bottled up inside him. He's not going to vent it on me again, and he's not going to vent it on my baby."

"All right, I understand. I'm poking my nose in where it doesn't belong."

"No, you're not. My mind is made up, that's all."

"Fair enough. Now, I was promised lunch, and I'm starving. Where's the food?"

"Step this way," Ann said, leading Joan to the dining area near the window.

Heath hung up the phone and glanced at the date at the top of the notepad on his desk.

Ten days. His baby was due in ten days.

He picked up the phone again and dialed the Jensen's home number. Joan answered on the fourth ring.

"Joan, it's Heath."

"Something told me I might be hearing from you today," Joan said dryly.

"How is she?"

"Ann is fine."

"How does she look?"

"Pregnant. Very pregnant."

"I mean, does she seem well?"

"Yes."

"Happy?"

Joan hesitated.

"Is she happy?" Heath insisted.

"She's happy about the baby, that much is true. I know she misses you."

"Did she say that?"

"Heath, you are not going to conduct an interrogation over the phone. I'm sorry Joe told you I was going to New York, I knew this would happen when I got back."

"You can't expect me to be indifferent. Ann's having my child, isn't she?"

"There was a time when you didn't think so."

"Joan, please. Without the acid commentary, are you sure she's okay?"

"Yes, Heath, she's fine."

"Do you think she might let me come and see the baby when it's born?"

The plaintive note in his voice almost broke Joan's heart. "I'm sure she wouldn't keep you out, Heath. You're the father."

"I don't know. She's pretty fed up with me."

"You could take legal action to see the child."

"I don't want to start throwing writs at her, that's not the way to win her back."

"Is that what you want?"

"It's what I've wanted since she moved to New York."

"Then do what she asks."

"Go into counseling?" he said derisively.

"Why not?"

"That's for screwups like Ann's brother."

"People can be screwed up in different ways. Ann says that Tim is doing very well in this rehabilitation program."

"He'd better, if he wants to stay out of jail."

"You should have an equally powerful incentive."

"I'm not a gambler, for God's sake. Is that where you think I belong, in group gripe sessions with druggies and drinkers and people who can't stay away from the roulette wheel?"

"I think you have to do something," Joan said.

"No, thanks."

"Then you can stay where you are and watch Ann raise your son from fifteen hundred miles away."

"Stop lecturing me, Joan." Then, "My son?"

"I'm sorry, I let that slip."

"It's a boy?"

"Yes."

There was a long silence.

"Heath, are you still there?"

"I wonder what he'll look like."

"There's only one way to find out," Joan said, and hung up the phone.

Heath was left with the dial tone blaring in his ear.

"Well, here I am, with boiling water," Amy said, sticking her suitcase through the door and then stepping over it. "Should I don the rubber gloves now?"

"Take it easy, Amy, nothing is happening yet."

"What a disappointment. I take my vacation time to spend it with you in your hour of need, and you're just standing there, looking like the fat lady in the circus."

"Thanks."

Amy patted Ann's chubby cheek. "Only kidding."

"It's a sensitive subject. I've gained thirty-five pounds."

"Good! You were too skinny."

"I'd defy anybody to say that now."

Amy put her suitcase on the sofa and unlocked it, producing a triplicate box of rubber pants, infant size.

"Did I come prepared?" she said, raising one brow.

"I'm impressed."

Amy, looking slim and tanned in shorts and a halter top, sat back on the sofa and tucked her legs under her.

"Why do they always talk about boiling water for the childbirth scenes in those old movies?" Amy inquired. "What the hell is it for, anyway?"

"Damned if I know," Ann replied. "Sterilization?"

Amy shrugged. "Seriously, kiddo, how are you feeling?" she asked.

"Huge."

"What does your doctor say?"

"She says that everything seems fine and I should be able to have a natural, successful labor."

"Good." Amy bit her lip, opened her mouth, then closed it again abruptly.

"Go ahead. You can ask," Ann said.

"Have you heard from him?"

"Just through the lawyer, Caldwell. Have you seen him in Florida?"

"On television."

"On television?" Ann asked.

"Some charity drive. I feel like telling him that charity begins at home."

Ann held up her hand to forestall the commentary. "I know, I know. But I want to ask you a favor."

"Shoot."

"Will you call him when the baby's born? He'll want to know and there's really nobody else I trust who'll be on the scene."

"What about Tim?"

"He's under house arrest until he completes his twelve-step program."

"If I talk to Heath, I can't promise civility."

"Amy, be nice."

"Why? Has Heath been nice?"

"This is a circular argument, Amy, and it's giving me more indigestion than I already have. Just call him, okay?"

"Okay."

"Now let's talk about something else."

"Have you picked out any boy's names you like?" Amy inquired brightly.

"No. I guess I'm superstitious. I want to make sure the baby's all right before I even think about names."

Amy got up and pressed Ann's hand warmly. "The baby will be all right," she said. "But I think that now we should move on to the really important discussion, the one that concerns my dinner date last Friday night."

"Who is he?"

"The personnel V.P."

"At your company? Uh-oh."

"We're keeping it a secret."

"Good luck. He's not married?"

"Newly divorced."

"How newly?"

"The decree was final three weeks ago."

"Oh, Amy, you'd better be careful."

"Don't you want to hear about the date?"

"Sure," Ann said. She sat and propped her feet up on a hassock, noting the degree of swelling in her ankles.

Not too bad, but it was still early in the day.

Ann folded her hands over her protruding belly and settled in to listen.

Three days later, at 2:00 a.m., Ann struggled off her bed and waddled out into the living room, where Amy was sleeping on the fold-out sofa.

"Amy, wake up!" Ann said, shaking her friend's shoulder aggressively.

Amy sat up, her hair over one eye.

"Wassa madda?" she mumbled.

"My water broke," Ann said.

"Wassit mean?"

"It means I have to get to the hospital right now. Will you call a cab while I get dressed?"

Amy stumbled to her feet and then into the kitchen, where she splashed cold water on her face and then returned, looking more alert but somewhat alarmed.

"Where's the number?" she asked.

"On the pad by the phone."

"I guess this is really happening," she said as Ann returned to the bedroom.

I guess it really is, Ann thought, and went to the closet for her clothes.

* * *

"He is just beautiful," Amy said to Joan, beaming, peering into the isolette as she stood next to the Jensens. The baby responded by opening his mouth in a toothless yawn and beating the air with two tiny red fists.

"You know who he looks like," Joan said.

"Like Heath with blue eyes," Amy replied.

"They all have blue eyes at the beginning."

"His will stay blue. He has Ann's eyes." Amy looked over at Joe. "I can't believe you got here before Heath."

"We were here for the weekend to see Joan's sister."

"Did you call him?" Joan asked Amy.

Amy nodded.

"What did he say?"

"He didn't say anything. He was already gone. His secretary told me that he had planned to be here for the due date."

"Then he should be walking through that door any minute," Joe observed.

The elevator doors parted and Heath stepped into the hall, carrying a large armload of roses wrapped in a florist's green waxed paper.

"You could make money with your psychic powers," Amy said to Joe.

"Remember that we all promised to be pleasant," Joan said archly.

Heath looked at the little group standing at the nursery window and hesitated, then took a deep breath. He was wearing light summer slacks and a pale yellow polo shirt that emphasized his dark good

looks. He walked up beside Amy and stood looking
at the little plastic carrier with ''Bodine'' written on
the I.D. card. He didn't say a word, but Amy watched
his eyes fill with tears. He bent his head as they ran
silently down his face.

Amy felt her hostility toward him drain away, to be
replaced by an almost reluctant compassion. She
looked significantly at Joan, who took Joe's arm and
steered her husband away from the nursery and back
toward the nurses' station.

''I wanted to be here for the birth,'' Heath finally
said. His voice sounded congested, like he had a cold.

''You just missed it. She was a little early.''

''Is Ann all right?''

''She's fine.''

''And the baby?''

''Perfect.''

Heath closed his eyes, his carved profile a study in
regret. ''I don't deserve either of them.''

Amy found herself patting his arm. No wonder
Ann couldn't stay angry with him.

''I want to see Ann,'' he said.

''She's still sleeping.''

''Then I'll wait.'' He looked around him restlessly
for the visitors' lounge.

''The waiting room is just down the hall,'' Amy
said. ''I'll show you.''

He followed her to the sterile cubicle, which had a
gray-and-white tiled floor and plastic gray-and-blue
chairs. Heath sat in one of them and stared at the
floor, still clutching the flowers.

''Should I take those?'' Amy asked. ''I'll get
someone to put them in water.''

He handed them to her.

"Was she in a lot of pain?" he asked.

"I don't think so."

"I've heard labor is very painful," he said.

"Most women seem to survive it."

He wasn't listening.

"I think I'll just go see the Jensens. We were about to leave for lunch when you arrived. Do you want to join us?"

Heath didn't answer.

"Heath?"

He looked up, startled.

"Lunch?"

He shook his head. "I'll stay here."

Amy gave up and found the Jensens, who were lingering near the nurses' station.

"Let's go. He's in another world. I don't think he'll be focusing on anything until he sees Ann."

"Should I go talk to him?" Joe asked.

"I think it's better to leave him alone, Joe. It's obvious that he has a lot on his mind."

Amy gave the flowers to the aide assigned to Ann's room and the trio departed.

In the waiting room, Heath sat alone, his eyes fixed on the checkered floor.

When Amy returned to Ann's room two hours later, minus the Jensens, Ann was reading the tags on several arrangements of flowers that had been delivered to her room.

"Who from?" Amy asked.

"The blue and white carnations are from Tim, and the glads are from my editor. The jade plant is from Daniela and Victor."

"Where's Heath?"

Ann stared at her. "Heath?"

"Yes, he was here just before I left and he said he would wait until you woke up to visit you."

Ann looked away, her expression thoughtful.

"You didn't see him?" Amy asked in astonishment, looking around as if Heath might be lurking somewhere in the room.

Ann shook her head.

"I can't believe it. He had this huge bunch of roses and—" Amy stopped. "You mean, he just left?"

"Apparently so."

"Why on earth would he do that?"

"Lost his nerve?" Ann suggested softly.

"Heath? Never."

"You don't know him the way I do."

"That's true," Amy said archly.

"Did he see the baby?" Ann asked.

Amy nodded. "He was very touched, Annie."

"Not touched enough to stick around," Ann replied, shaking her head.

A nurse came into the room carrying a squalling bundle. "Somebody's hungry, Mother," she said.

Ann held out her arms and the nurse placed the baby in Ann's embrace. His little face was wrinkled and his eyes screwed shut as his lips worked furiously.

"Will you feed the kid, already?" Amy said. "He sounds like a fire siren."

"Healthy lungs," the nurse said approvingly.

Ann unbuttoned the top of her nightgown and pushed her nipple into the baby's mouth. He rooted frantically for a couple of seconds and then settled down to suck contentedly.

"You're pretty good at that," Amy said wonderingly, smiling.

"He does all the work," Ann replied.

"Did Mrs. Bodine's visitor leave?" Amy asked the nurse.

"Which one?"

"Her husband," Amy said dryly.

"That young man was Mr. Bodine?" the nurse said, surprised. "He never told me. He left about an hour ago. That reminds me, I'll go and get the flowers he brought."

Amy waited until the nurse had gone back into the hall before she said, "I'll never understand that man."

"Maybe he just wanted to see the baby, not me," Ann said dejectedly, looking down at her son.

"Oh, Annie, no. He really was concerned about you." Seeking to change the subject, she said, "What are you going to name that little one?"

"I don't know."

"It says Baby Boy Bodine on his isolette, maybe you can stick with that."

Ann smiled weakly at the feeble joke, then lifted the baby to her shoulder to burp him. After a few firm pats, he belched loudly.

"Healthy digestive system," the nurse confirmed as she entered the room again with Heath's flowers arranged in a vase and an ivy plant in her other hand.

"This place is starting to look like a greenhouse," Amy said, making room for the ivy on Ann's bedside stand. "Who's Ben Rowell?" she added, reading the card.

"One of Heath's employees."

"I guess you'll be getting a few more of those."

"Probably. I'll ask the staff to deliver them to a rest home or something."

They both looked up as Heath suddenly appeared in the doorway, his arms laden with a football, a basketball, and a pair of roller skates. The expression on his face as he saw his son nursing at Ann's breast was one she would never forget.

"I'll be back tonight, Ann," Amy said, heading for the door. She paused at Heath's side and kissed his cheek.

"Congratulations, Daddy," she said, and left.

"There's a sporting goods store across the street. I thought I'd kill a little time until you woke up," Heath said nervously by way of explanation.

"I think he's a little young for those, Heath."

"I know. I just wanted to do...something," he said lamely. He put down his burdens and pulled a chair next to the bed, watching wordlessly as the baby fed, making satisfied sucking noises.

"He has a good appetite," Heath said.

"Yes."

The baby's activity slowed as they looked on, fascinated. His jaws finally ceased motion altogether, his eyes closed and, in seconds, he was asleep.

"That fast?" Heath said.

"The nurse said they go out like lights at this stage." Ann settled the baby next to her on the bed and tucked his receiving blanket up to his chin.

When she looked back at Heath, he had slumped visibly and had put his head in his hands.

"Heath?" she said softly.

He looked up, took her free hand, and held it to his lips.

"Isn't your son beautiful?" Ann asked.

He nodded, swallowing painfully. Then, to Ann's complete amazement, Heath leaned forward to put his head in her lap and began to sob.

"I didn't want you to be alone through this," he said thickly. "I wanted all of it to be different."

"It's all right," Ann said, stroking his hair gently. "It's all over now."

"You don't understand." He lifted his head and she saw that his face was stained with tears.

Even when they were teenagers, she had never seen him cry.

"I thought so many times of calling you, but..." He gestured, unable to continue.

"What?" Ann prompted him.

"Even from the beginning, I wasn't sure you would want my baby, knowing what you knew about my family. I wasn't sure you would want me, or us, as a package..." He shook his head and stopped again. This was very difficult for him to say.

"I want the package," she said, "but—"

The nurse bustled into the room as Heath hastily turned his head away from her.

"Sleeping already?" she said, picking the baby up and feeling his bottom. "Still dry, too. Well, he'll just have a nice nap and then come back to visit this evening. Your son is a handsome fellow, isn't he, Mr. Bodine?"

"Yes," Heath replied, clearing his throat.

"I'm glad to see you. We thought you were missing in action earlier."

"Just a visit to the store," Ann said quickly, gesturing to the pile of toys on the chair.

"New fathers can never wait for the athletic equipment," the nurse said, chuckling as she left with the baby.

"What do I have to do to get some privacy here, rent out a whole ward?" Heath said disgustedly.

"It's a hospital, Heath. They run in and out constantly. There's nothing you can do."

"Yes, there is." He got up and closed the door. On the way back to her bed, he pulled his wallet from his pants pocket. He extracted two cards and handed them to her.

"I've joined a group called Adult Children of Alcoholics," he said. "That's the name and number of my partner. I've already attended two meetings."

Ann was speechless.

"And I contacted a doctor—a family counselor—on Big Palm. I had a first session with her. We have to go back together as soon as you're able. If you want to try again with me, that is." He looked at her warily, as if afraid she might say no.

"Of course I want to try," Ann said, touching his cheek, still in shock.

"I can't promise anything. Just going to see those people in the first place was hard."

"I'm sure it was."

"But I want...to get better," he said lamely.

"You will. Taking the initial step is the most difficult. The rest will be easier."

Heath dropped his head to her lap again, wrapping his arms around her legs, which were covered by the sheet.

Ann sank her fingers into his hair.

"I love you so much, Princess," he said, his voice partially muffled by the bedclothes.

"I love you, too, Heath."

"I'd like to name the baby after Joe, if it's okay with you, that is."

"What a nice idea."

"He's been more of a father to me than my biological father ever was."

"Joe and Joan will be thrilled."

"And Timothy, for your brother."

"Oh, Heath, he'll be so pleased. I think it will be just the lift Tim needs to get him through all this."

"So we'll both be in recovery programs, just different kinds," Heath said ruefully. "It looks like you're the only stable member of this outfit."

"And Joseph Timothy Bodine. We'll make sure that he is very stable."

"That's a promise," Heath said, twining his fingers with hers tightly.

Ann smiled at him and then closed her eyes.

"Tired?" he said.

"A little."

"Go back to sleep. I'll be here when you wake up."

Ann sighed deeply and turned her head on the pillow, relaxing into sleep.

Still holding her hand, Heath settled in to wait.

*   *   *   *   *

Get Ready to be Swept Away by
Silhouette's Spring Collection

Abduction
&
Seduction

These passion-filled stories explore both the dangerous
desires of men and the seductive powers of women.
Written by three of our most celebrated authors, they are
sure to capture your hearts.

Diana Palmer
Brings us a spin-off of her Long, Tall Texans series

Joan Johnston
Crafts a beguiling Western romance

Rebecca Brandewyne
New York Times bestselling author
makes a smashing contemporary debut

Available in March at your favorite retail outlet.

MILLION DOLLAR SWEEPSTAKES (III)

No purchase necessary. To enter, follow the directions published. Method of entry may vary. For eligibility, entries must be received no later than March 31, 1996. No liability is assumed for printing errors, lost, late or misdirected entries. Odds of winning are determined by the number of eligible entries distributed and received. Prizewinners will be determined no later than June 30, 1996.

Sweepstakes open to residents of the U.S. (except Puerto Rico), Canada, Europe and Taiwan who are 18 years of age or older. All applicable laws and regulations apply. Sweepstakes offer void wherever prohibited by law. Values of all prizes are in U.S. currency. This sweepstakes is presented by Torstar Corp., its subsidiaries and affiliates, in conjunction with book, merchandise and/or product offerings. For a copy of the Official Rules send a self-addressed, stamped envelope (WA residents need not affix return postage) to: MILLION DOLLAR SWEEPSTAKES (III) Rules, P.O. Box 4573, Blair, NE 68009, USA.

EXTRA BONUS PRIZE DRAWING

No purchase necessary. The Extra Bonus Prize will be awarded in a random drawing to be conducted no later than 5/30/96 from among all entries received. To qualify, entries must be received by 3/31/96 and comply with published directions. Drawing open to residents of the U.S. (except Puerto Rico), Canada, Europe and Taiwan who are 18 years of age or older. All applicable laws and regulations apply; offer void wherever prohibited by law. Odds of winning are dependent upon number of eligibile entries received. Prize is valued in U.S. currency. The offer is presented by Torstar Corp., its subsidiaries and affiliates in conjunction with book, merchandise and/or product offering. For a copy of the Official Rules governing this sweepstakes, send a self-addressed, stamped envelope (WA residents need not affix return postage) to: Extra Bonus Prize Drawing Rules, P.O. Box 4590, Blair, NE 68009, USA.

SWP-S295

INTIMATE MOMENTS®
Silhouette®

WOUNDED WARRIORS

Men and women hungering for passion to soothe their lonely souls. Watch for the new Intimate Moments miniseries by

Beverly Bird

It begins in March 1995 with

A MAN WITHOUT LOVE (Intimate Moments #630)
Catherine Landano was running scared—and straight into the arms of enigmatic Navaho Jericho Bedonie. Would he be her savior...or her destruction?

Continues in May...

A MAN WITHOUT A HAVEN (Intimate Moments #641)
The word *forever* was not in Mac Tshongely's vocabulary. Nevertheless, he found himself drawn to headstrong Shadow Bedonie and the promise of tomorrow that this sultry woman offered. Could home really be where the heart is?

And concludes in July 1995 with

A MAN WITHOUT A WIFE (Intimate Moments #652)
Seven years ago Ellen Lonetree had made a decision that haunted her days and nights. Now she had the chance to be reunited with the child she'd lost—if she could resist the attraction she felt for the little boy's adoptive father...and keep both of them from discovering her secret.

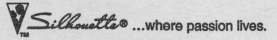

Silhouette® ...where passion lives.

BBWW-1

Hot on the heels of **American Heroes** comes
Silhouette Intimate Moments' latest and greatest
lineup of men: **Heartbreakers.** They know who
they are—and *who* they want. And they're out to
steal your heart.

RITA award-winning author Emilie Richards kicks off
the series in March 1995 with *Duncan's Lady,* IM #625.
Duncan Sinclair believed in hard facts, cold reality
and his daughter's love. Then sprightly Mara MacTavish
challenged his beliefs—and hardened heart—with
her magical allure.

In April *New York Times* bestseller Nora Roberts
sends hell-raiser Rafe MacKade home in
The Return of Rafe MacKade, IM #631. Rafe had
always gotten what he wanted—until Regan Bishop
came to town. She resisted his rugged charm and
seething sensuality, but it was only a matter of time....

Don't miss these first two **Heartbreakers,** from two
stellar authors, found only in—

HRTBRK1

Southern **Knights**

Join Marilyn Pappano in March 1995 as her **Southern Knights** series draws to a dramatic close with *A Man Like Smith*, IM #626.

Federal prosecutor Smith Kendricks was on a manhunt. His prey: crime boss Jimmy Falcone. But when his quest for justice led to ace reporter Jolie Wade, he found himself desiring both her privileged information—and the woman herself....

Don't miss the explosive conclusion to the **Southern Knights** miniseries, only in—

KNIGHT3

EXTRA! EXTRA! READ ALL ABOUT...
MORE ROMANCE
MORE SUSPENSE
MORE INTIMATE MOMENTS

Join us in February 1995 when
Silhouette Intimate Moments introduces
the first title in a whole new program:
INTIMATE MOMENTS EXTRA. These break-
through, innovative novels by your favorite
category writers will come out every few
months, beginning with Karen Leabo's
Into Thin Air, IM #619.

Pregnant teenagers had been
disappearing without a trace, and
Detectives Caroline Triece and Austin Lomax
were called in for heavy-duty damage
control...because now the missing girls
were turning up dead.

In May, Merline Lovelace offers
Night of the Jaguar, and other
INTIMATE MOMENTS EXTRA novels will
follow throughout 1995, only in—

THE
MEN OF
MIDNIGHT

RITA award-winning author Emilie Richards launches her new miniseries, **The Men of Midnight,** in March 1995 with *Duncan's Lady,* IM #625.

Single father Duncan Sinclair believed in hard facts and cold reality, not mist and magic. But sprightly Mara MacTavish challenged his staid beliefs—and hardened heart—with her spellbinding allure, charming both Duncan and his young daughter.

Don't miss **The Men of Midnight,** tracing the friendship of Duncan, Iain and Andrew—*three men born at the stroke of twelve and destined for love beyond their wildest dreams,* only in—

INTIMATE MOMENTS®
Silhouette

MENM1